DIFFERENT SEASONS

Grimm Fairy Tales: Different Seasons Adult Coloring Book Volume 1, September, 2016. First Printing. Published by Zenescope Entertainment Inc., 433 Caredean Drive, Ste. C, Horsham, Pennsylvania 19044. Zenescope and its logos are ® and © 2015 Zenescope Entertainment Inc. all rights reserved. Grimm Fairy Tales, its logo and all characters and their likeness are © and ™ 2015 Zenescope Entertainment. Any similarities to persons (living or dead), events, institutions, or locales are purely coincidental. No portion of this publication may be reproduced or transmitted, in any form or by any means, without the expressed written permission of Zenescope Entertainment Inc. except for artwork used for review purposes. Printed in USA.

ARTWORK BY:

ANTONIO BIFULCO
JENEVIEVE BROOMALL
FRANCHESCO!
EMILIO LAISO
DAWN MCTEIGUE
MARAT MYCHAELS
RICHARD ORTIZ
PAOLO PANTALENA
ALE GARZA
MANUEL PREITANO
MICHAEL DOONEY

SEAN CHEN
MIKE KROME
JOE PEKAR
ALFREDO REYES
AL RIO
EDGAR SALAZAR
NOAH SALONGA
SEAN SHAW
ANTHONY SPAY
HARVEY TOLIBAO
BILLY TUCCI
JAMIE TYNDALL

PRODUCTION & DESIGN: ASHLEY VANACORE & CHRISTOPHER COTE
MANAGING EDITOR: JENNIFER BERMEL

WWW.ZENESCOPE.COM

Joe Brusha President & Chief Creative Officer
Christopher Cote Art Director
Pat Shand Writer & Editor
Dave Franchini Assistant Editor
Jessica Rossana Assistant Editor
Joi Dariel Production Manager

John Lyons Director of Sales & Marketing
Jennifer Bermel Director of Business Development
Jason Condeelis Direct Market Sales & Customer Service
Stu Kropnick Operations Manager
Ralph Tedesco VP Film & Television

READY! SET! COLOR!

STEP ONE
Choose your favorite spooky drawing.

STEP TWO
Obtain your coloring instrument of choice.
(crayon, colored pencils, or markers)

STEP THREE
Start coloring! Resist the urge to look over your shoulder for vampires, ghosts, or denizens of the night. There's nothing there. Promise.

STEP FOUR
Have fun!

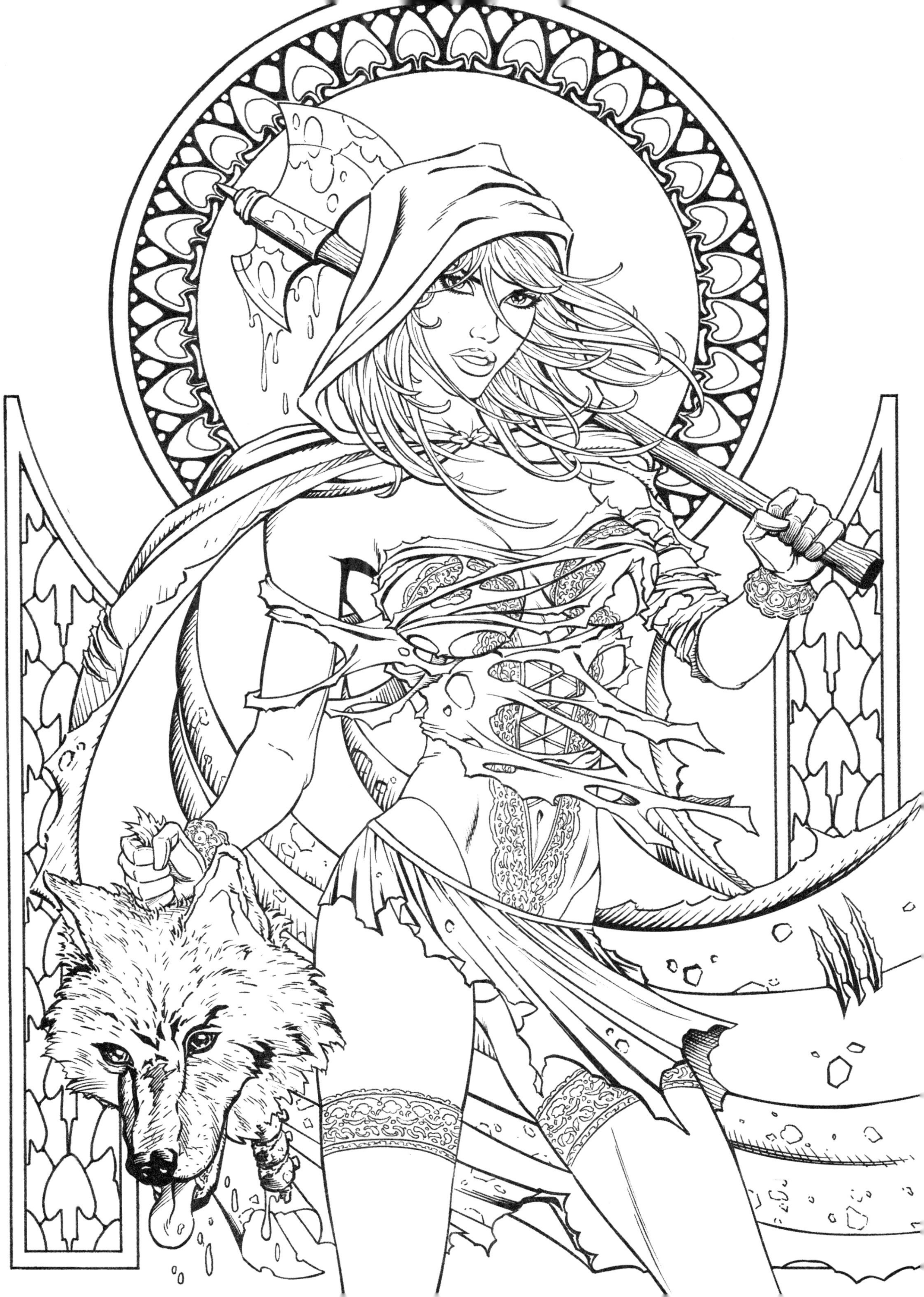

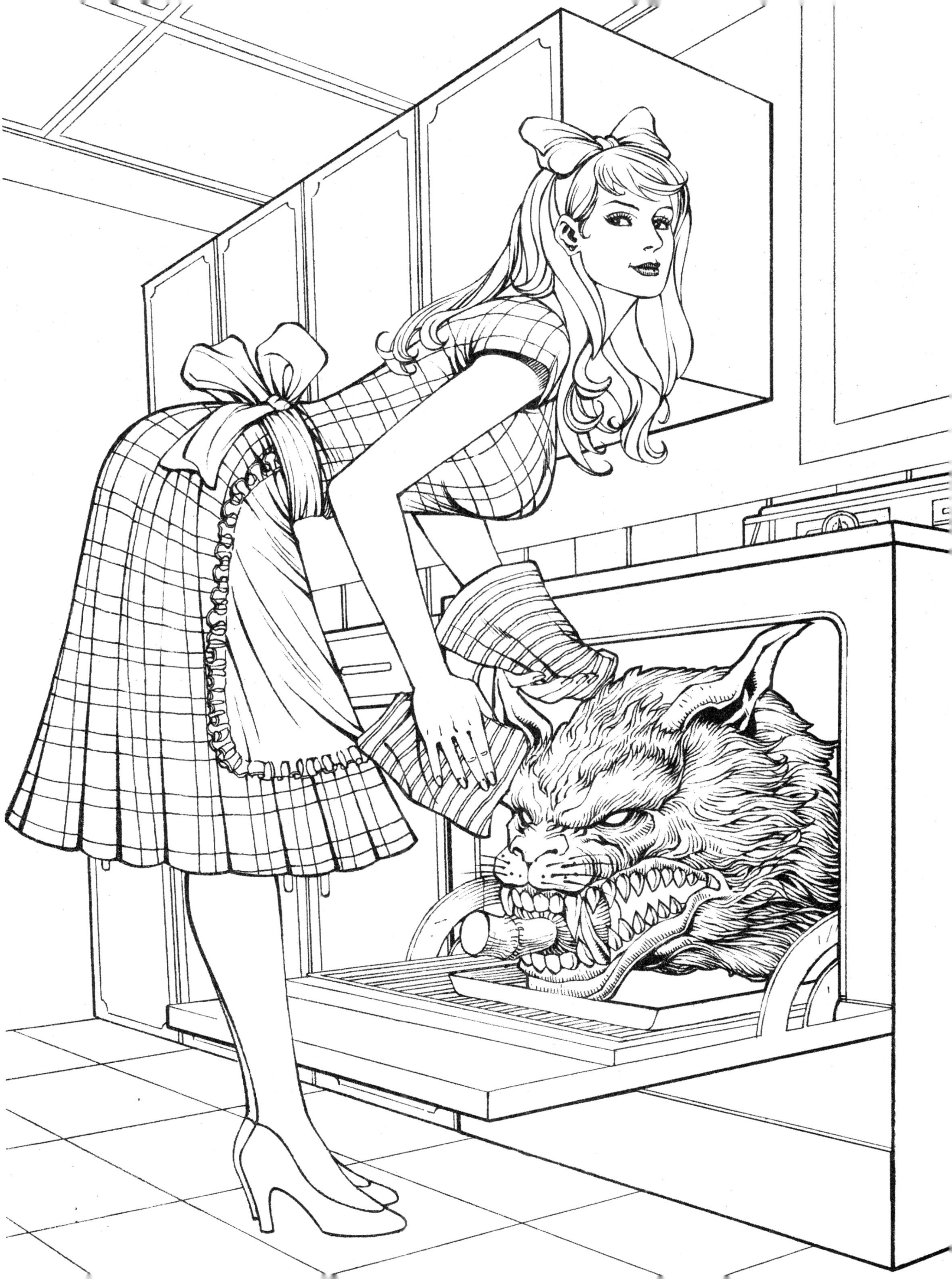

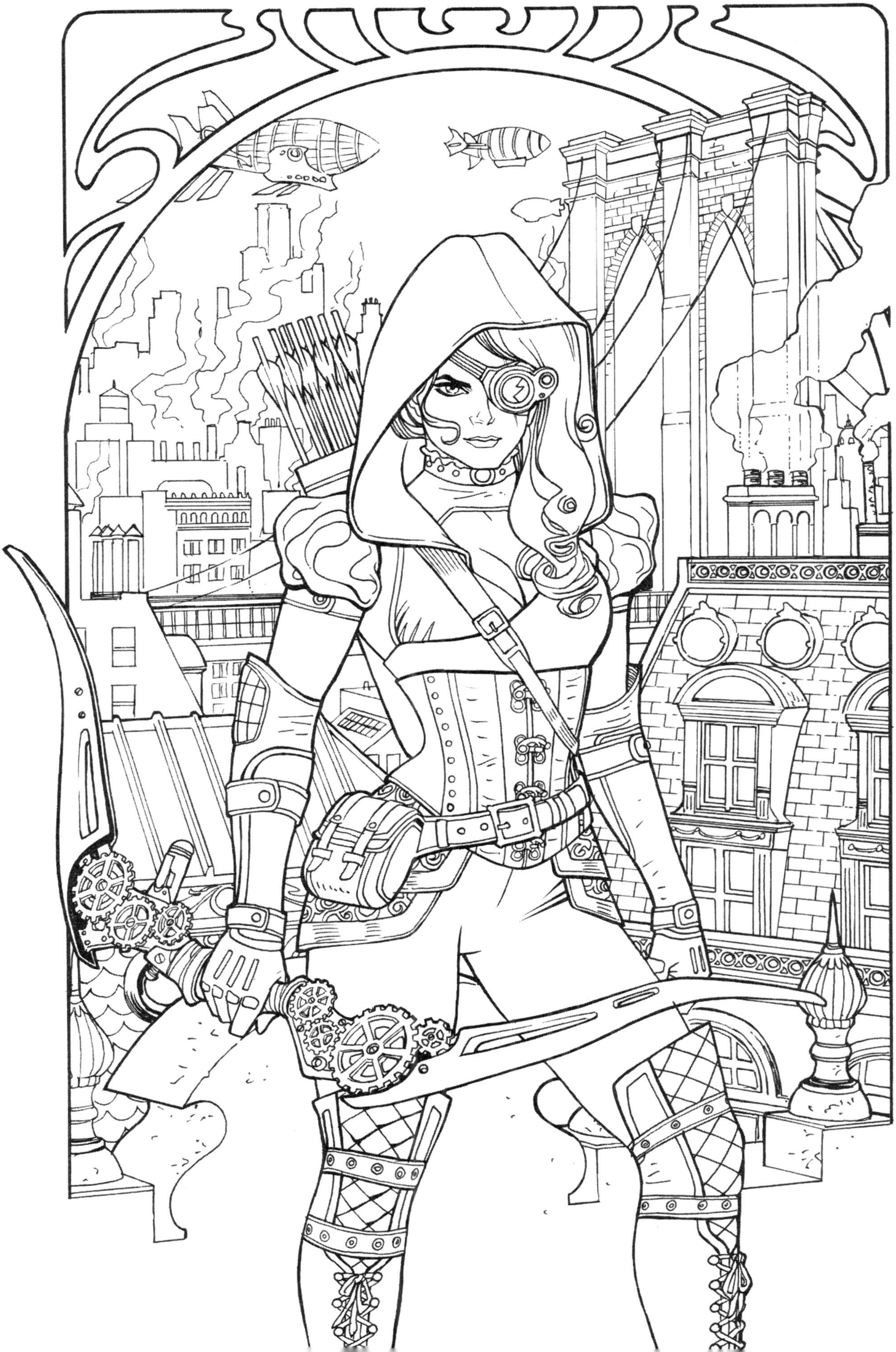

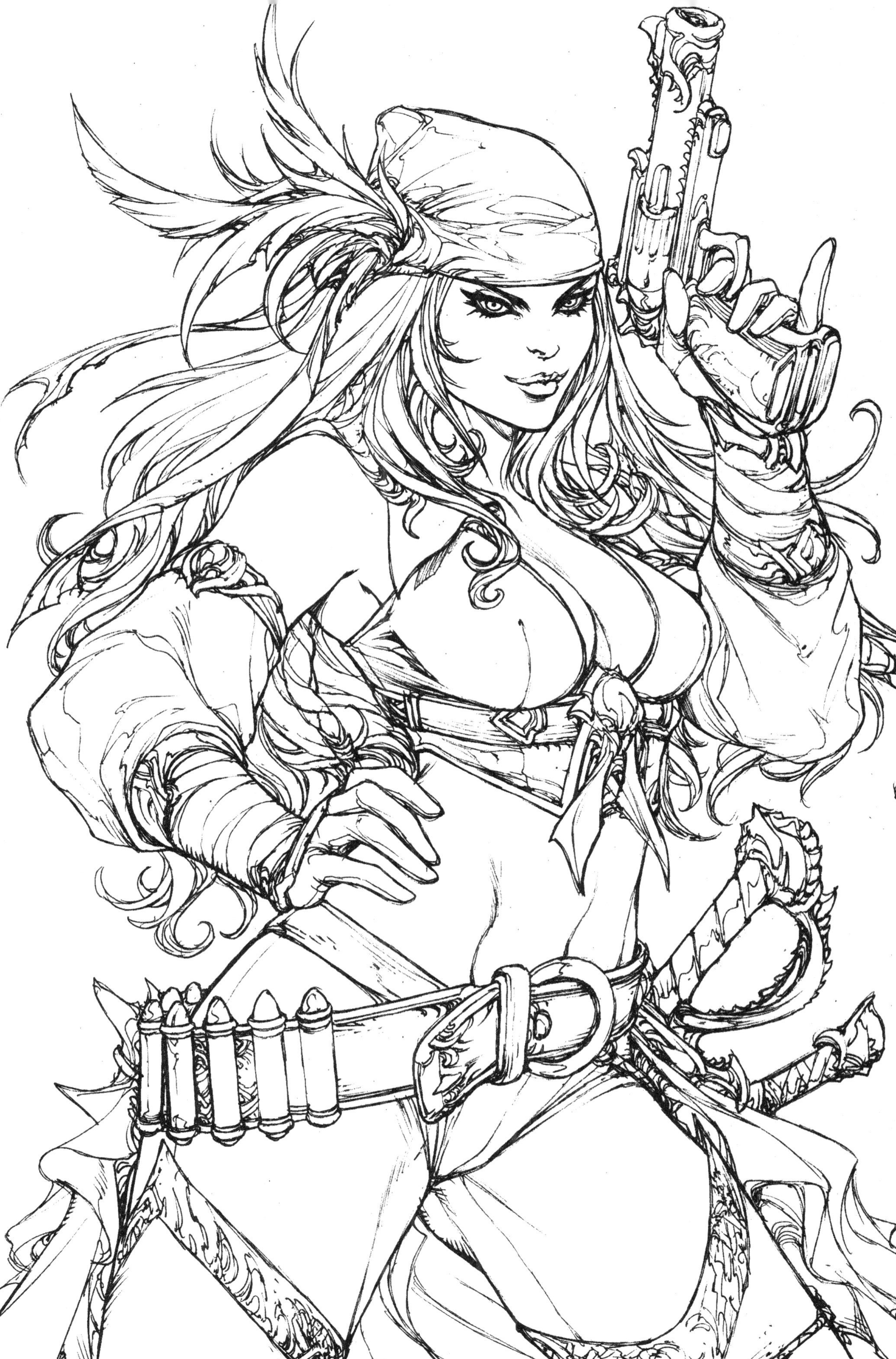

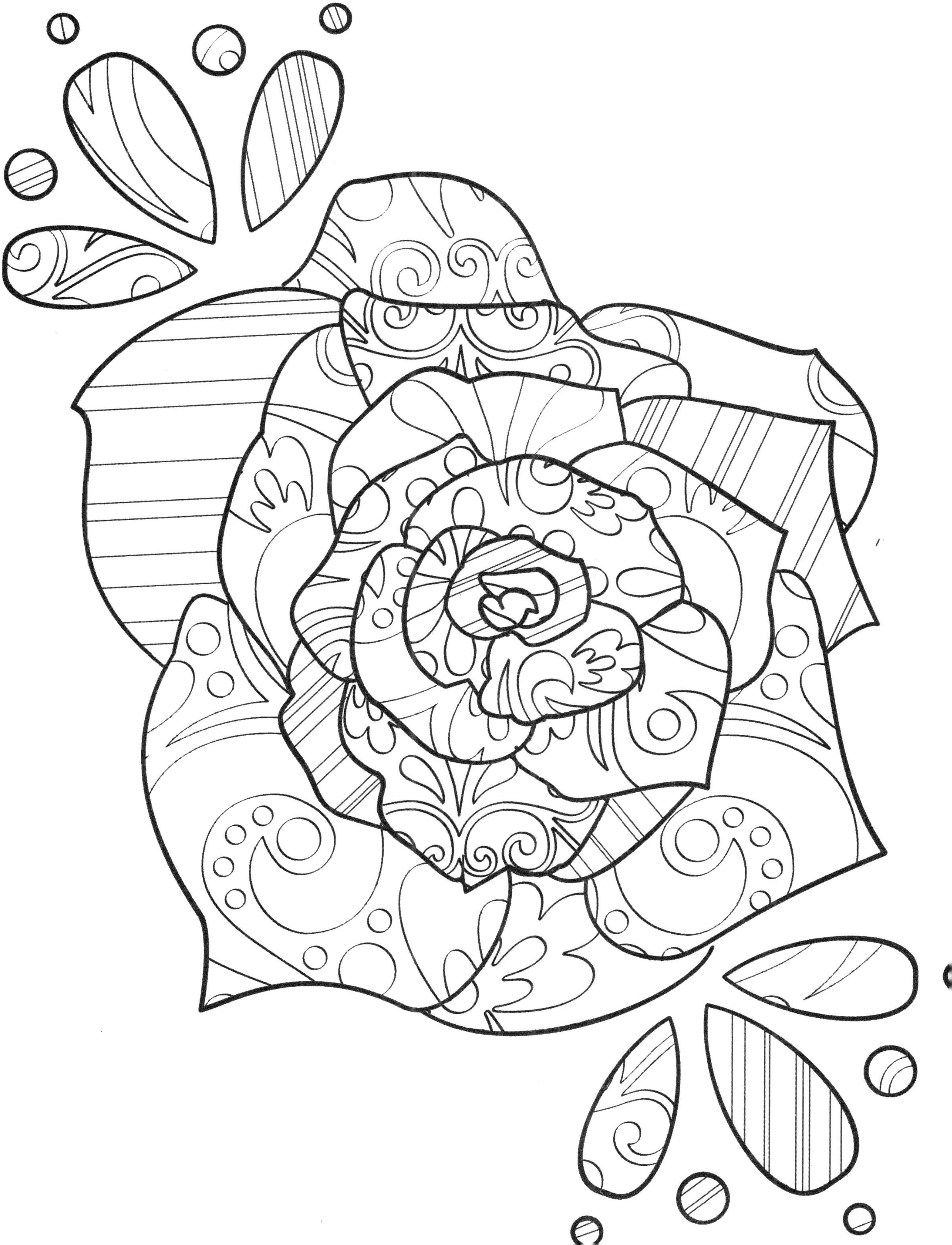

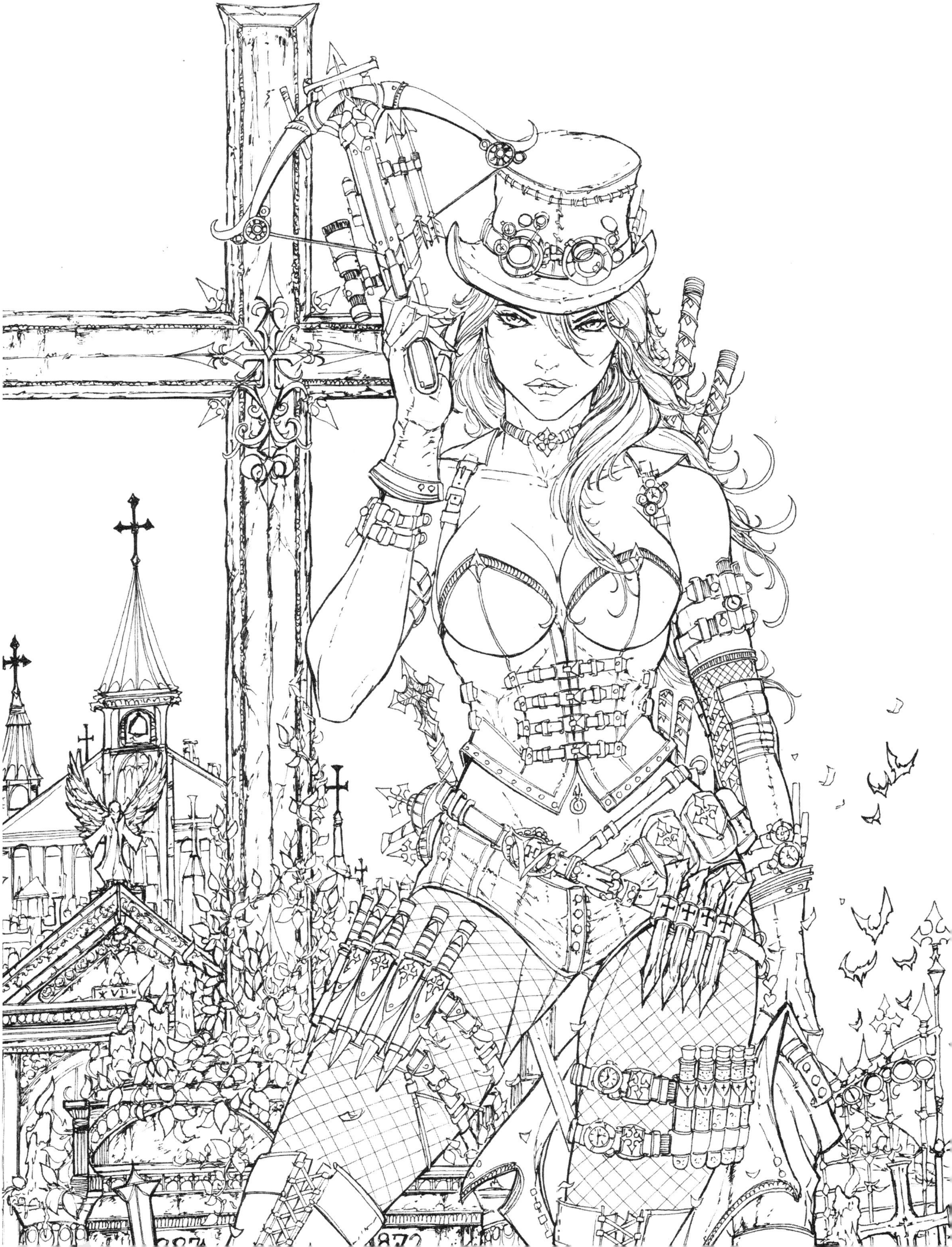

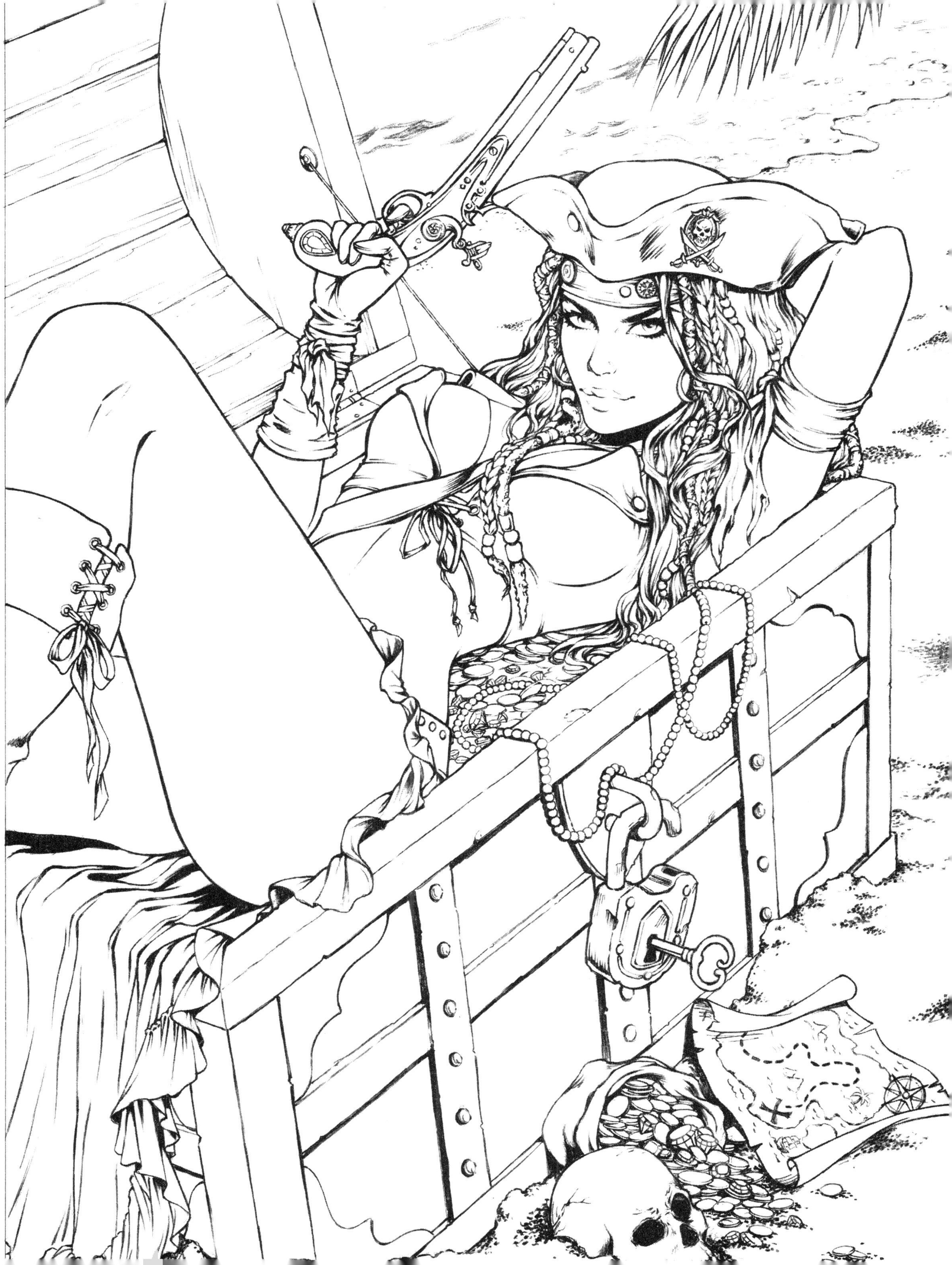

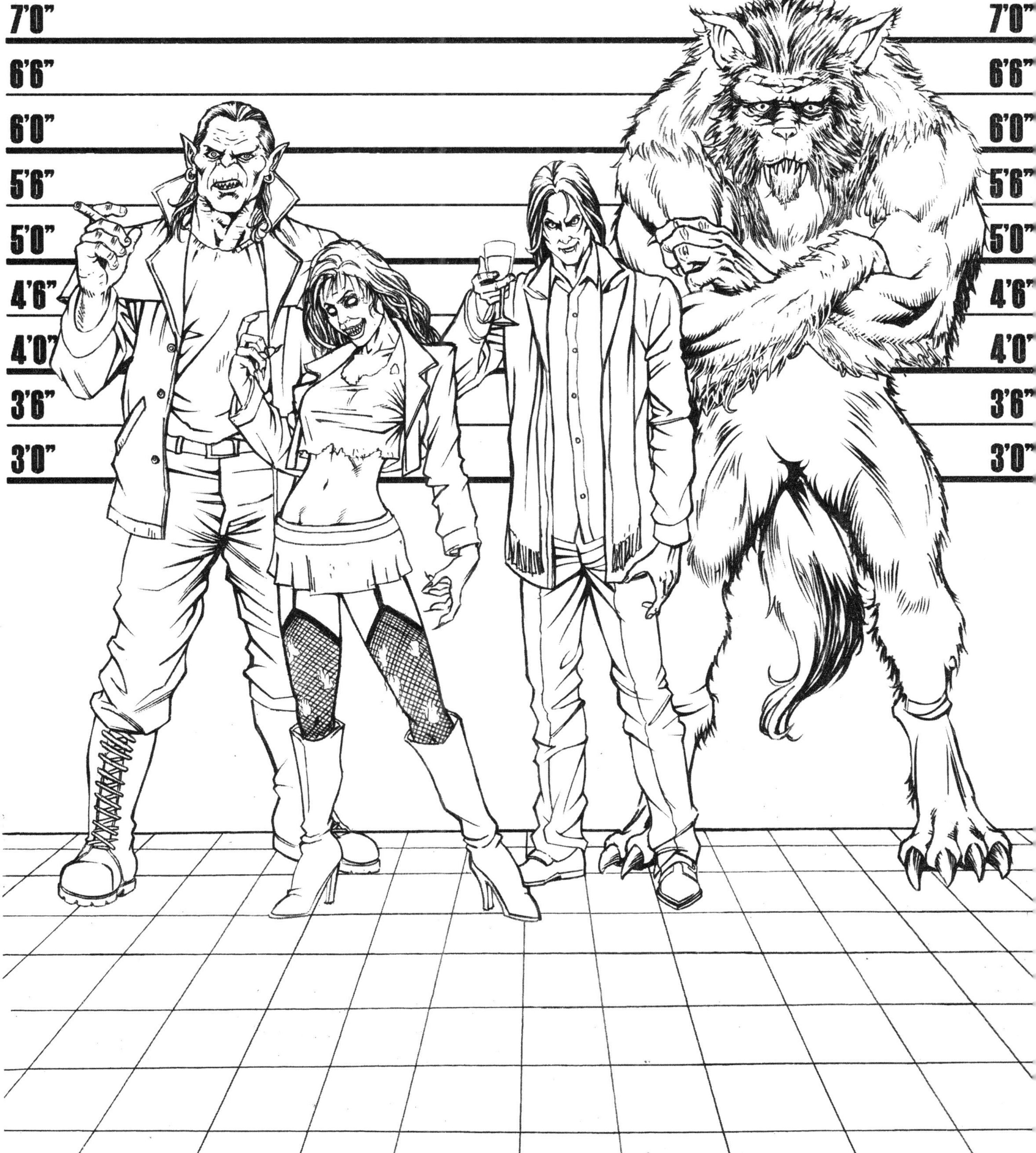
7'0"
6'6"
6'0"
5'6"
5'0"
4'6"
4'0"
3'6"
3'0"

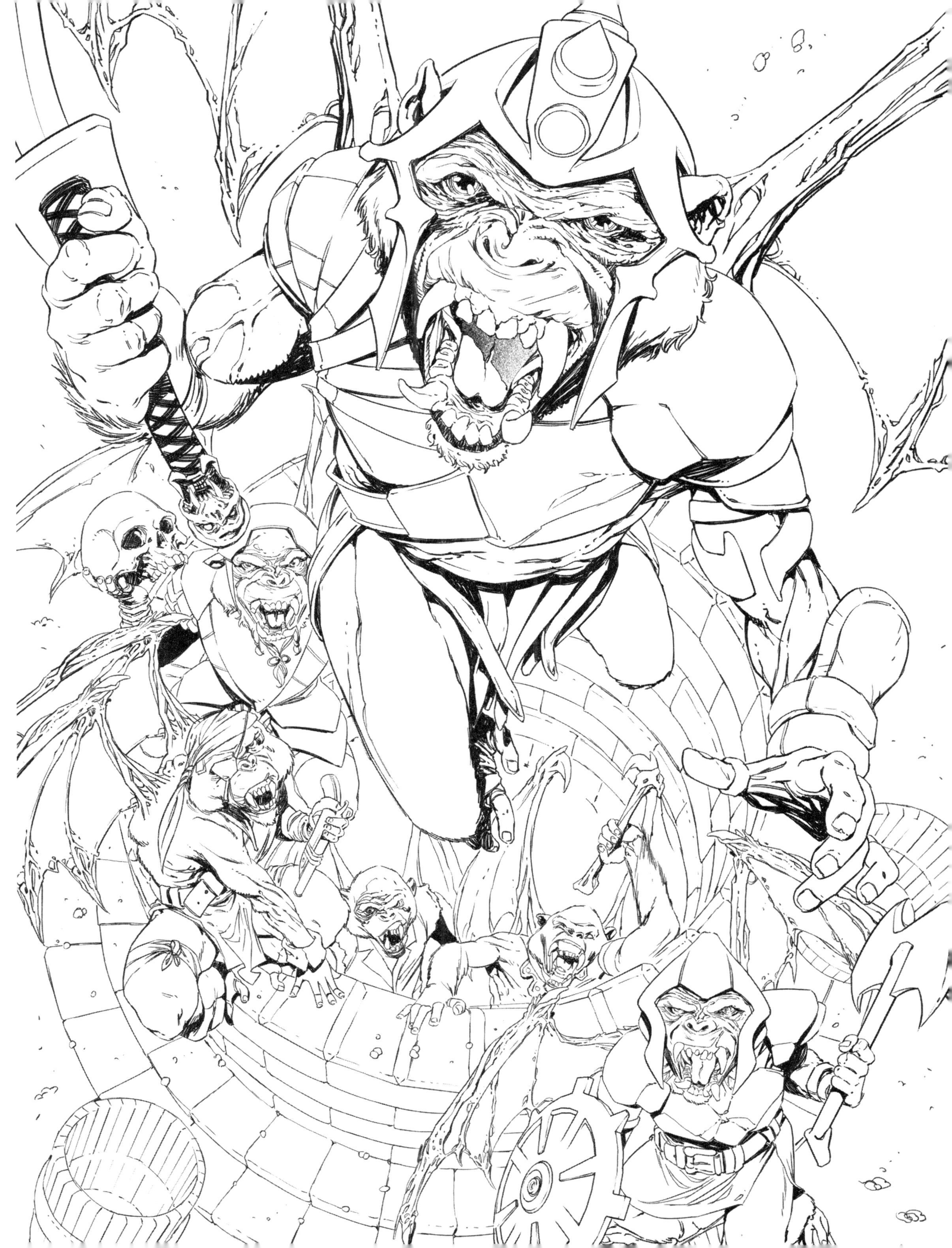

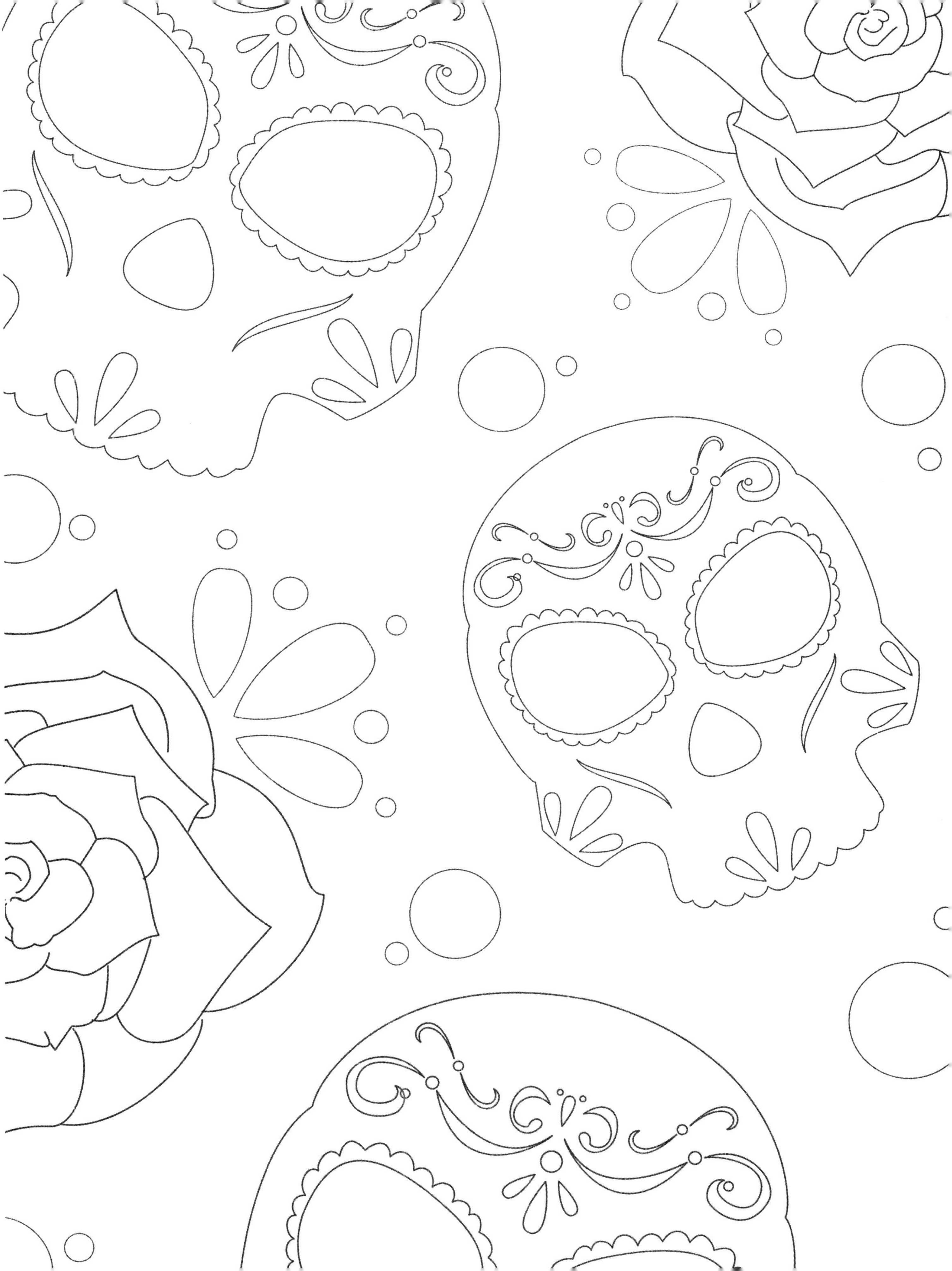

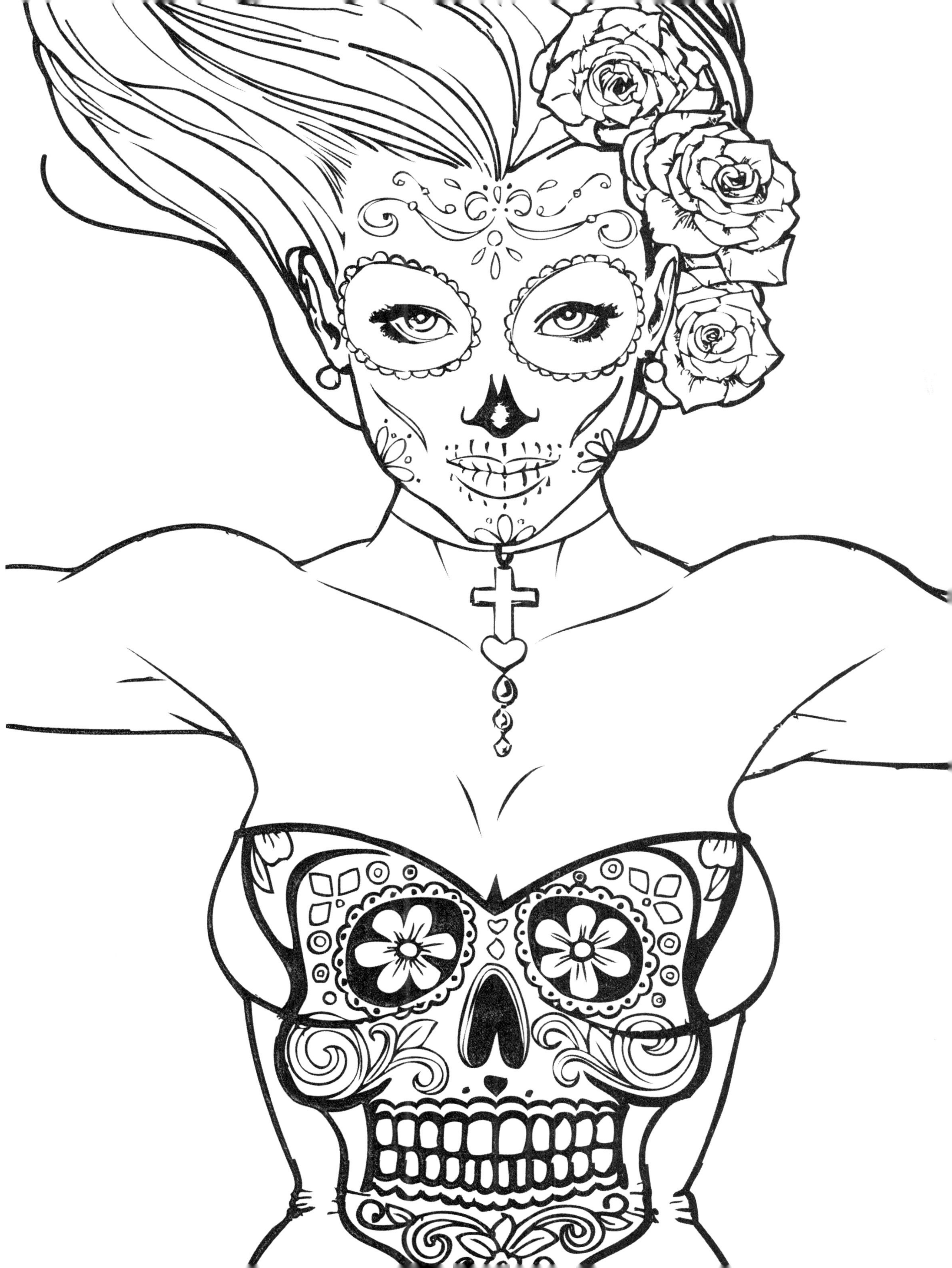

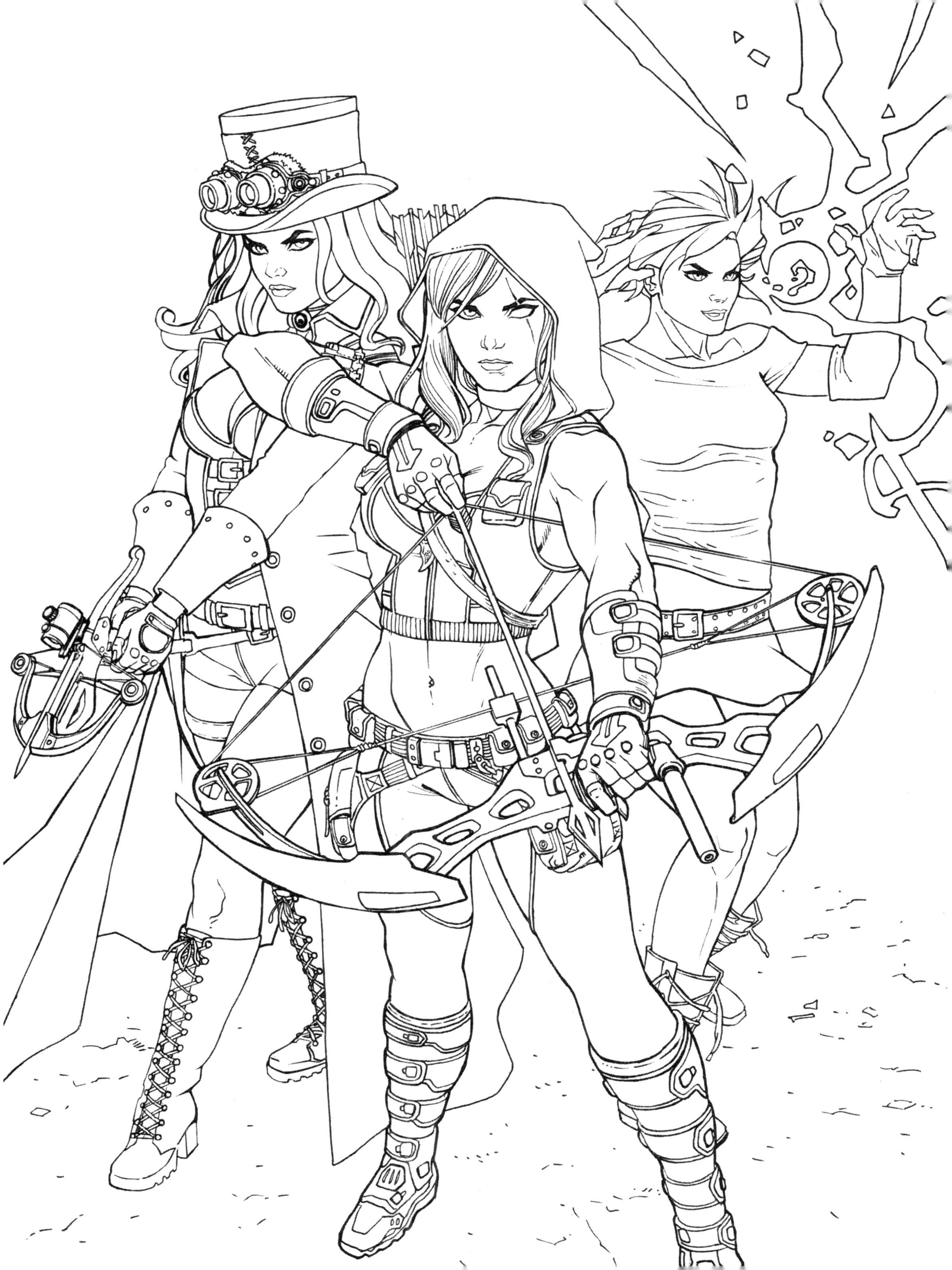

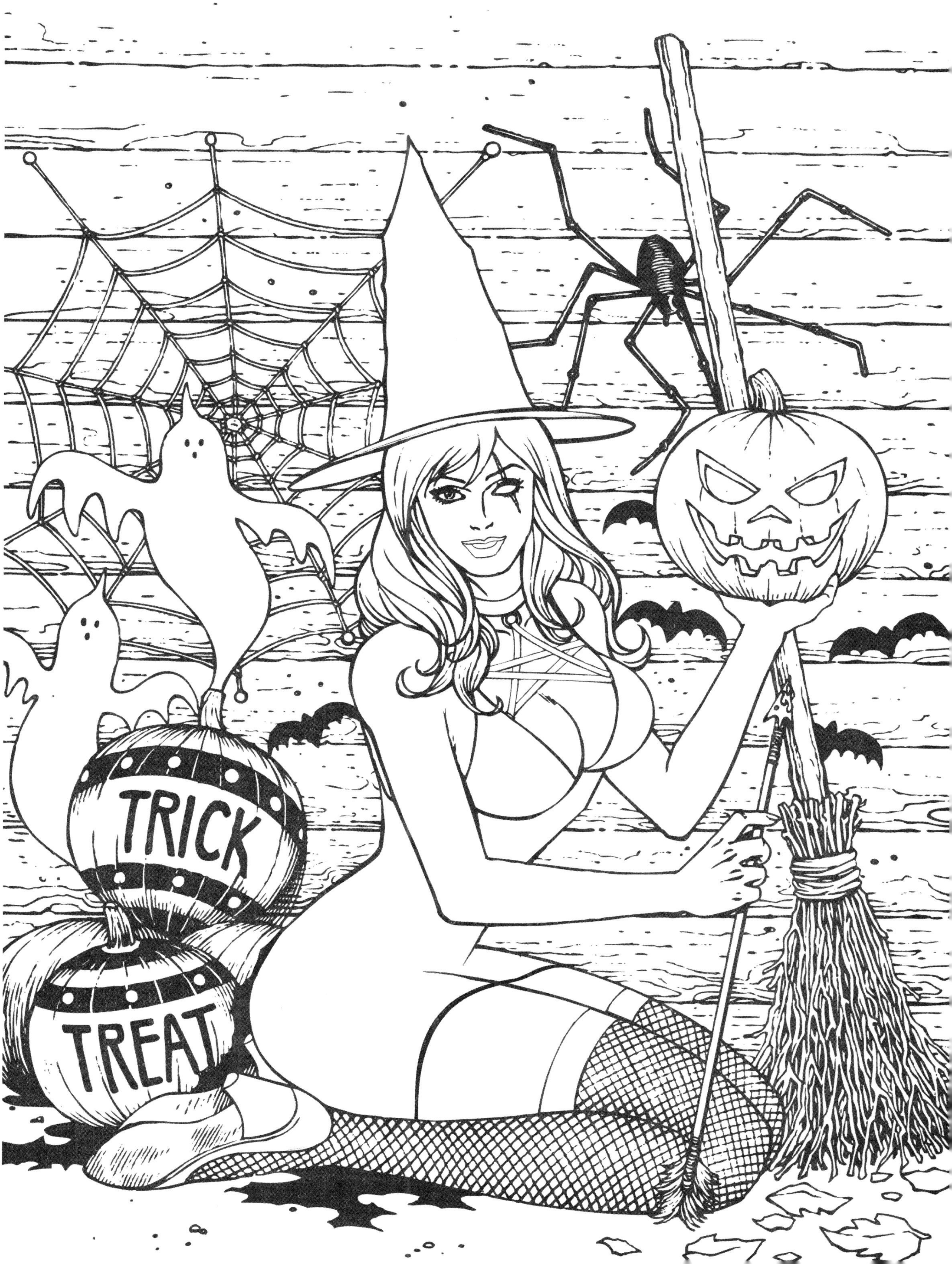
TRICK
TREAT

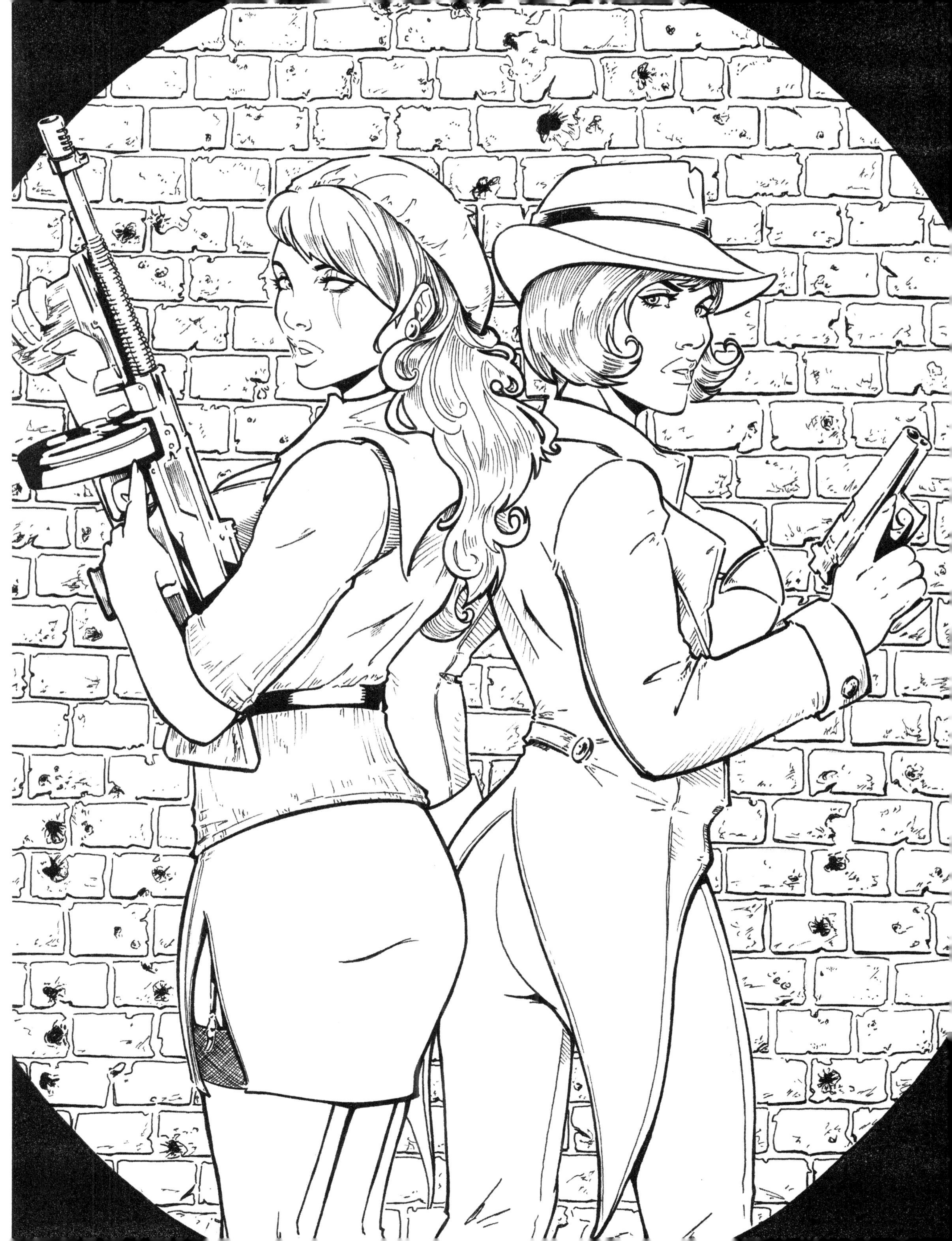

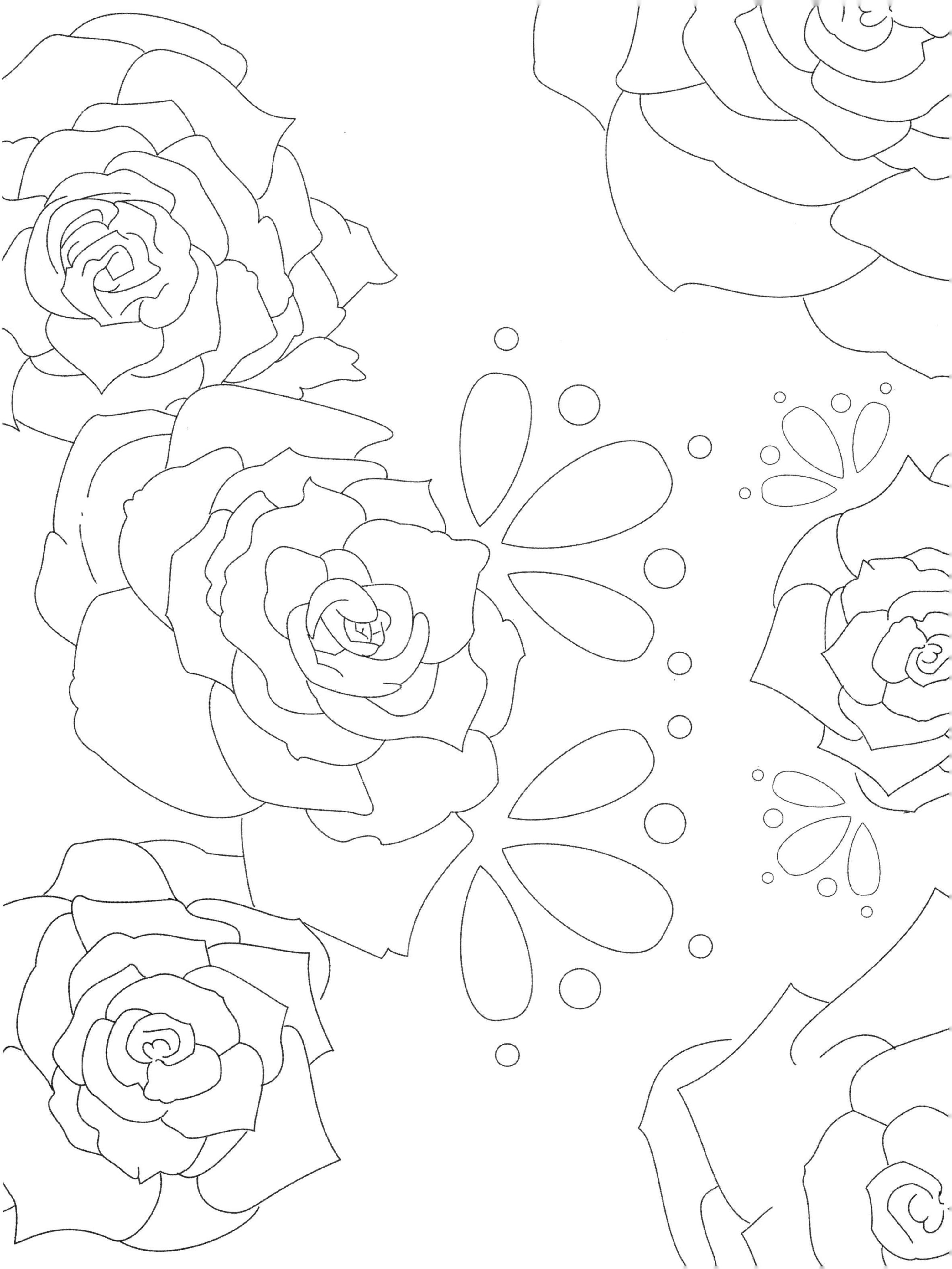

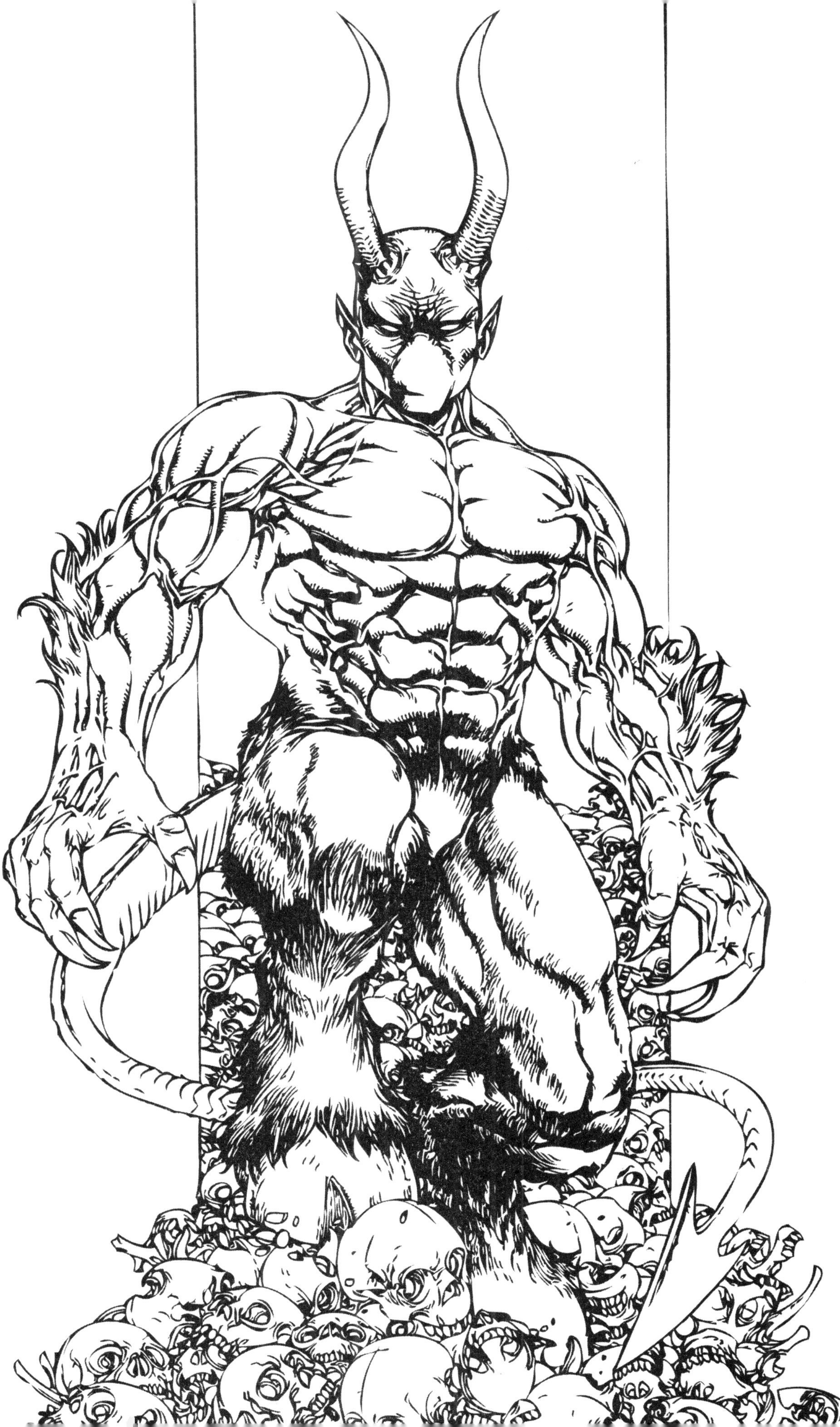

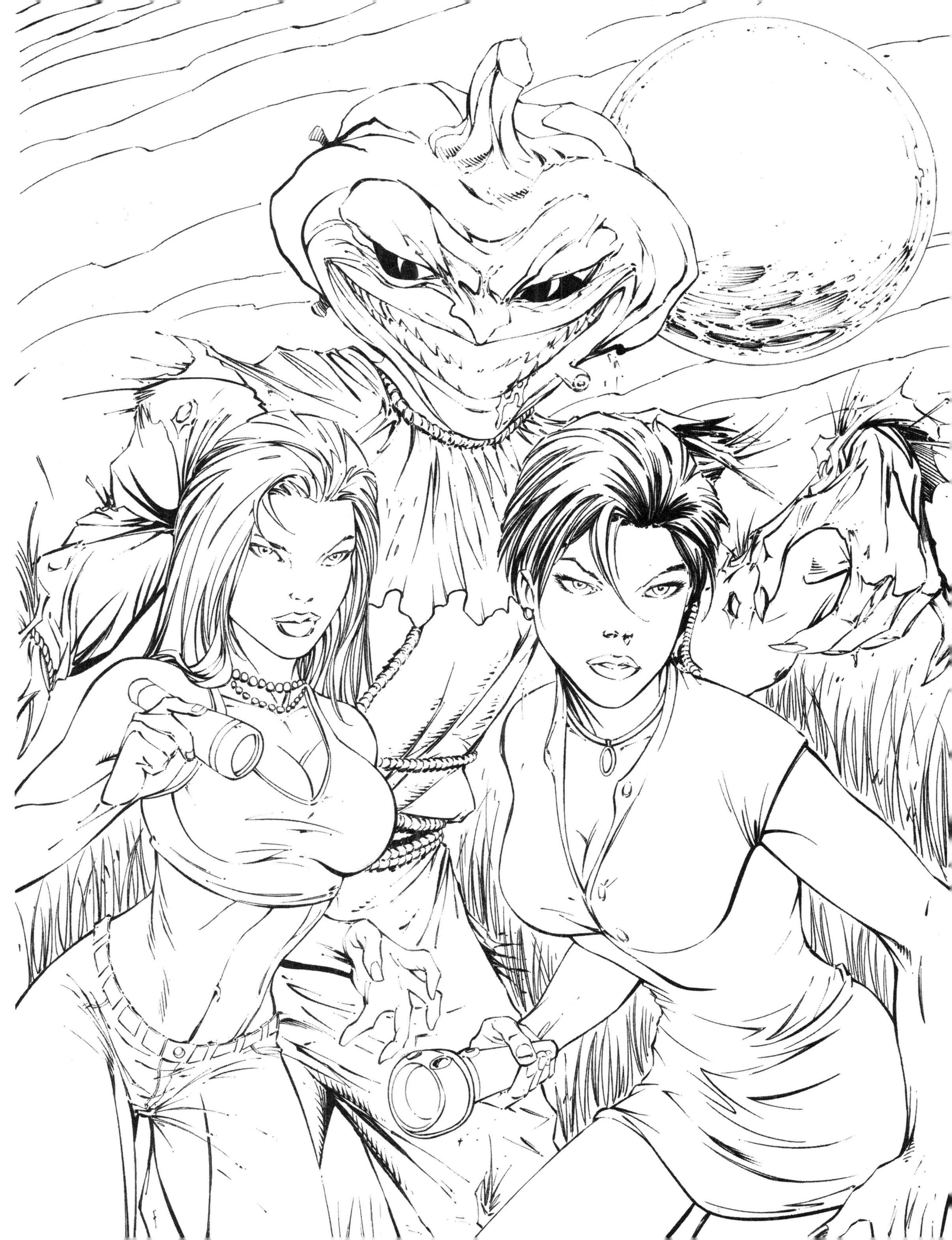

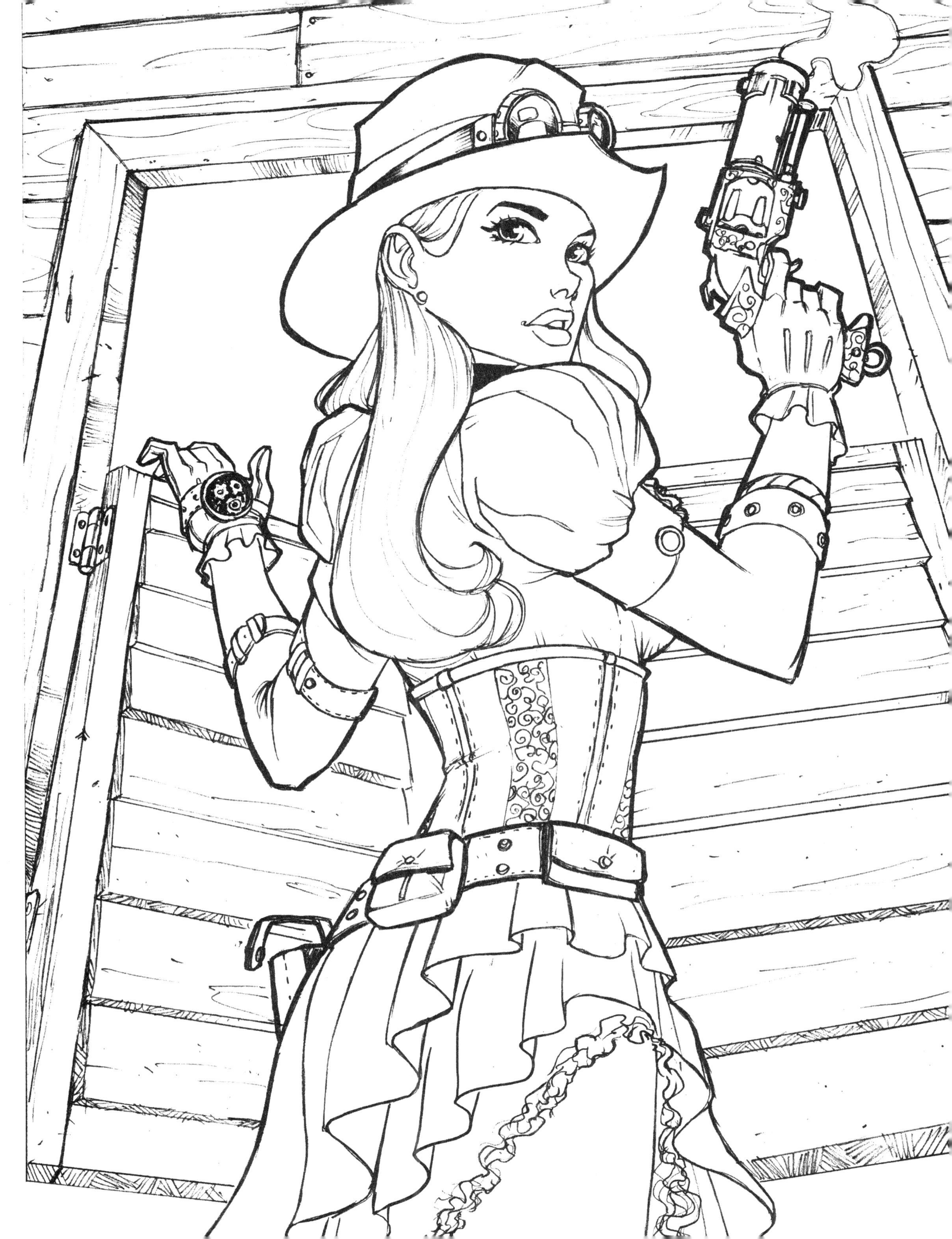

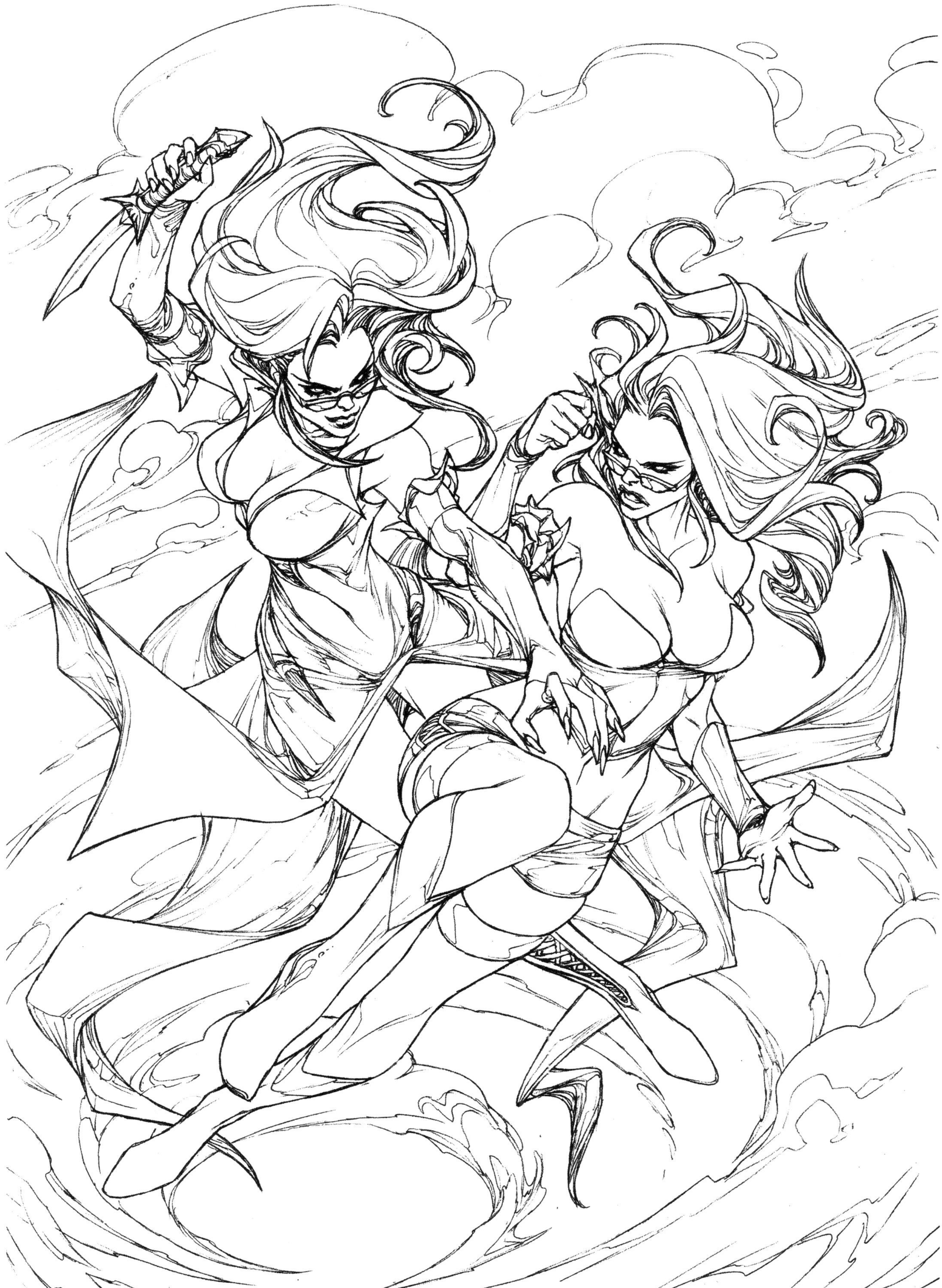

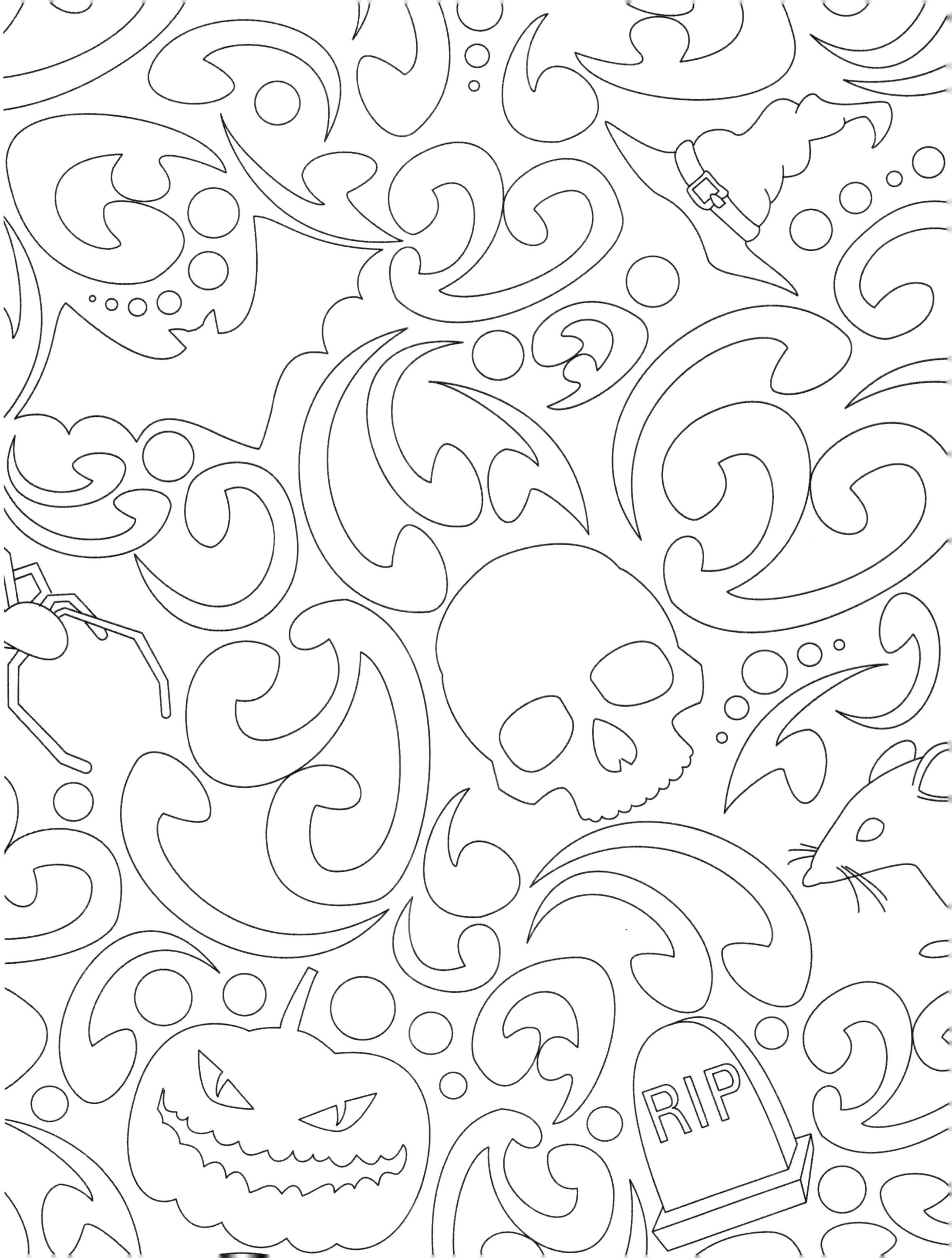
RIP

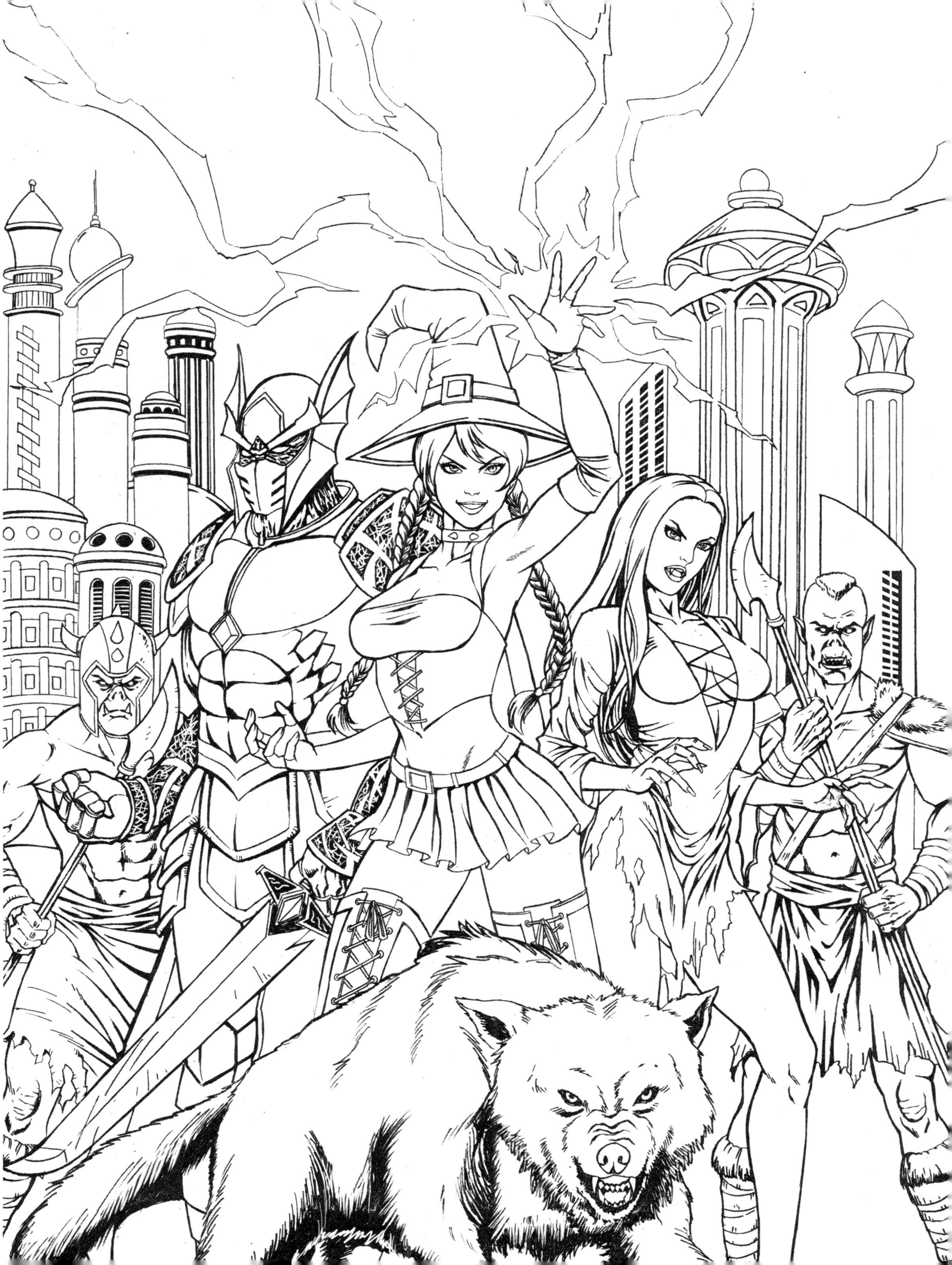

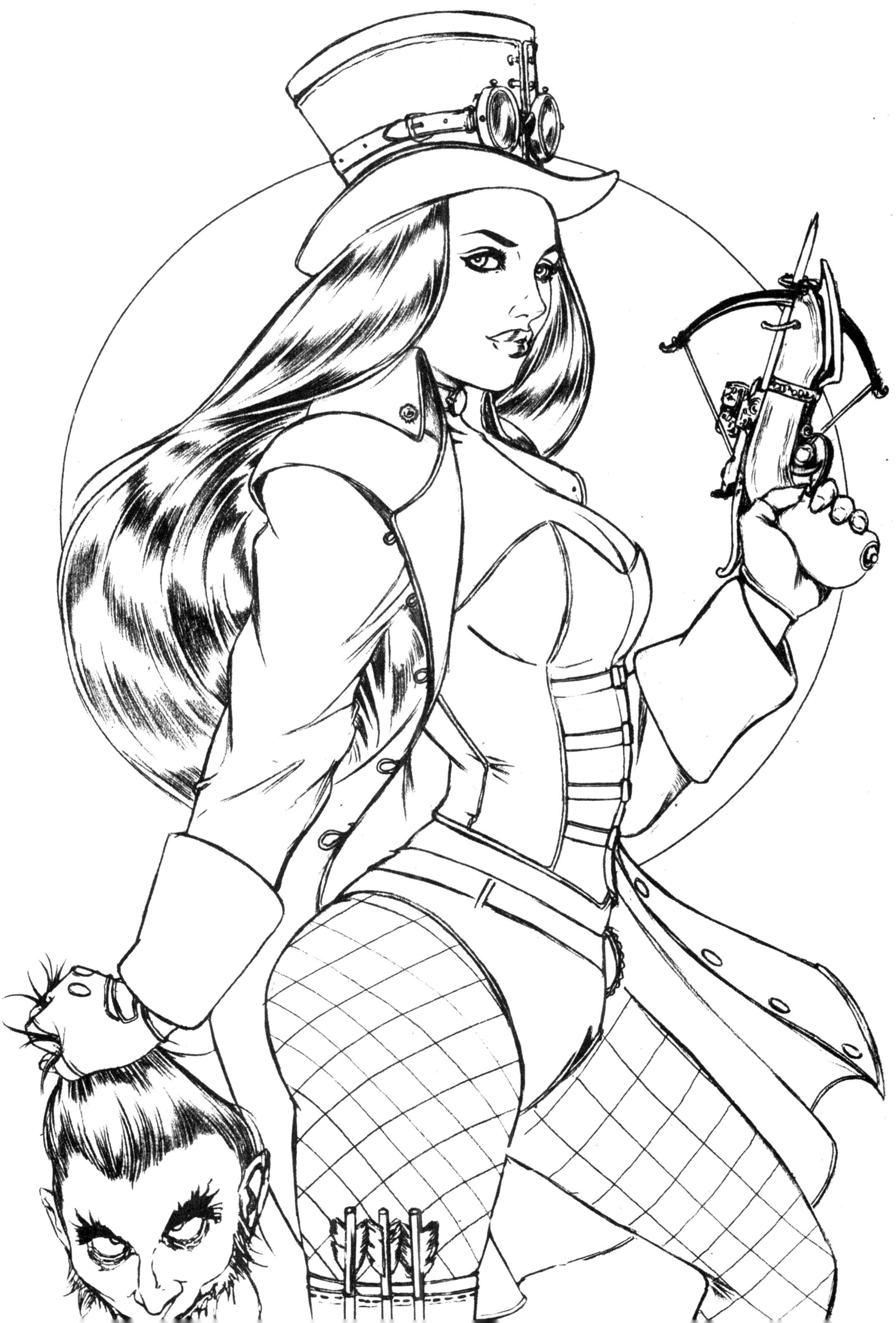

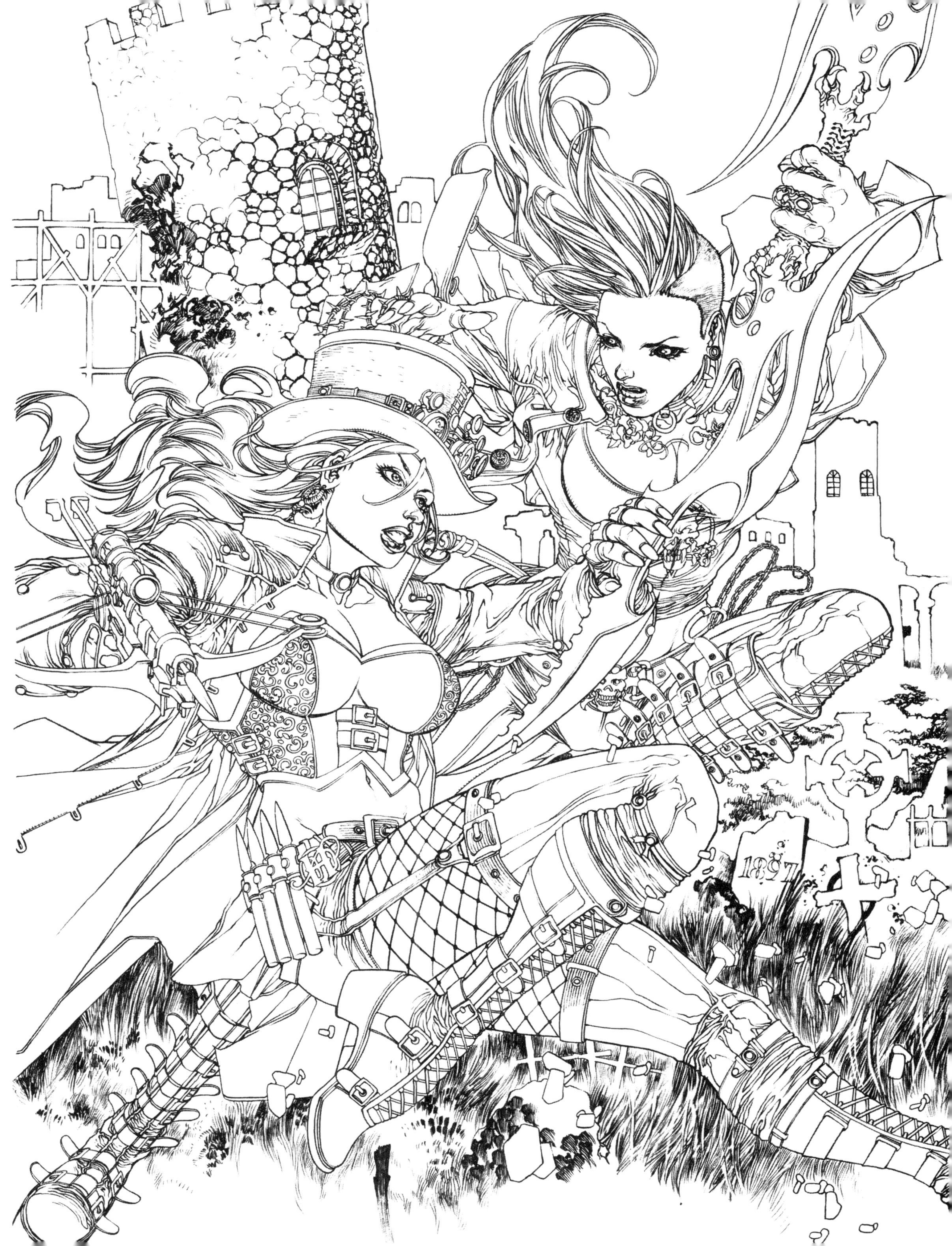
1897

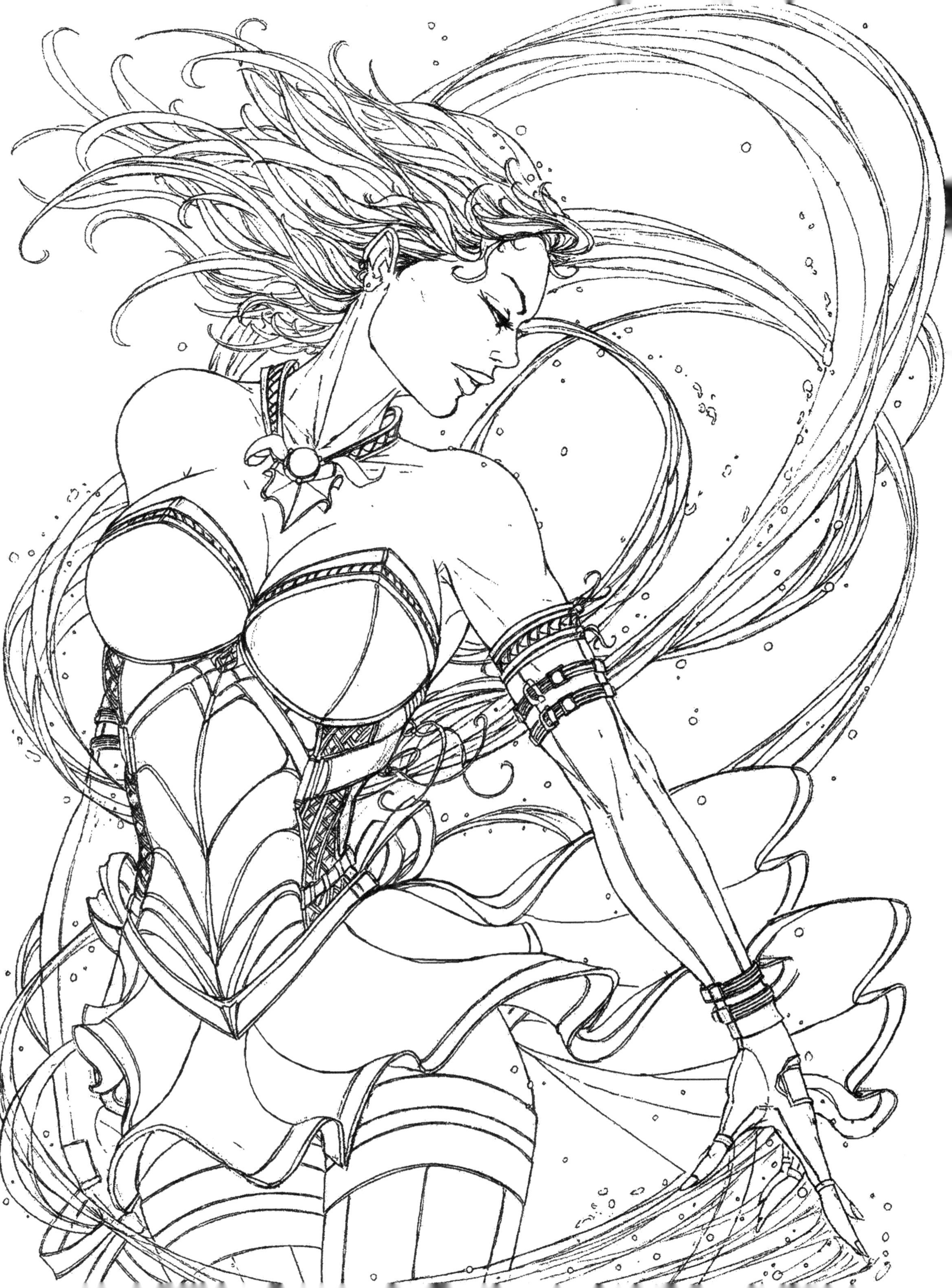

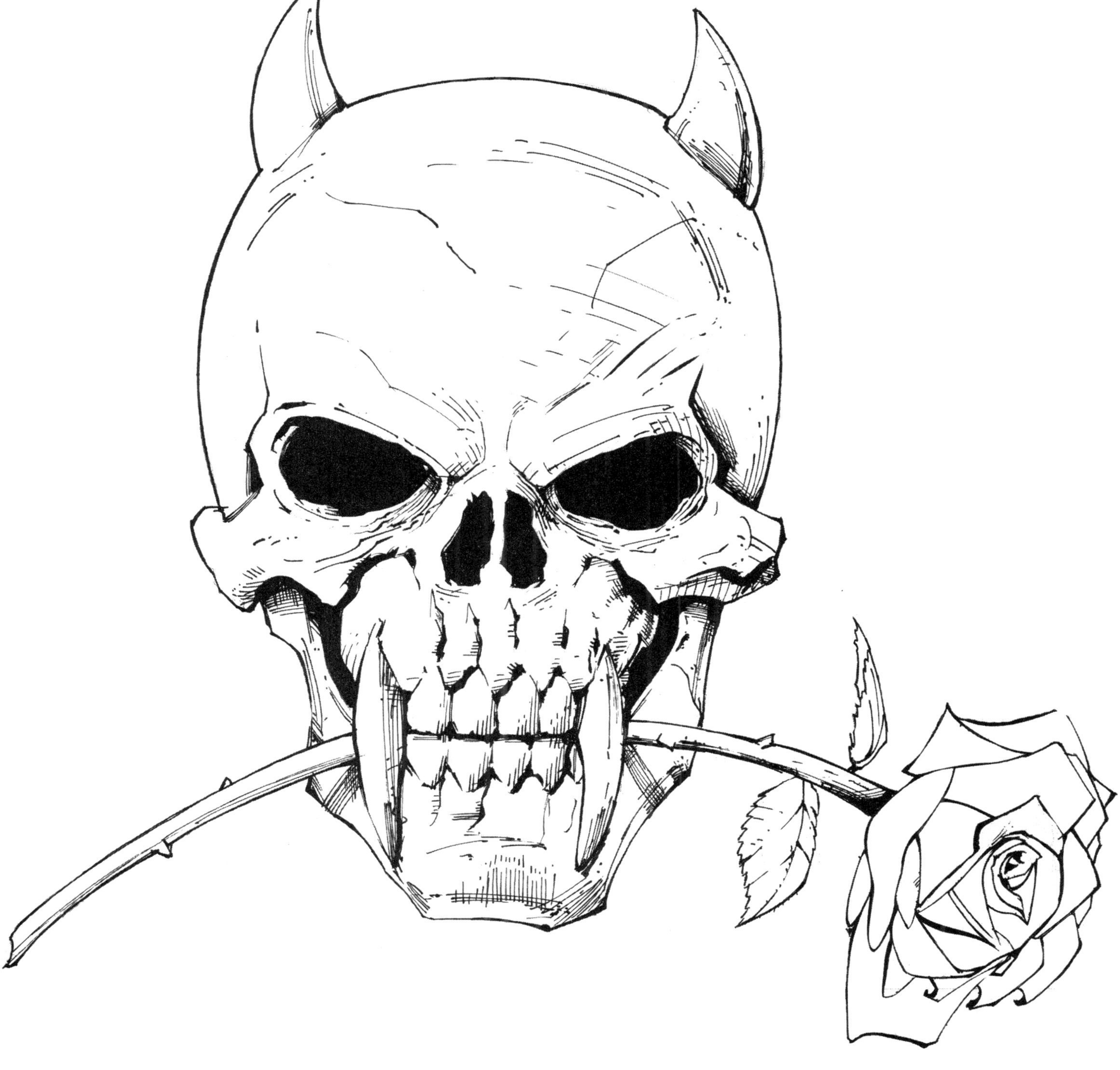

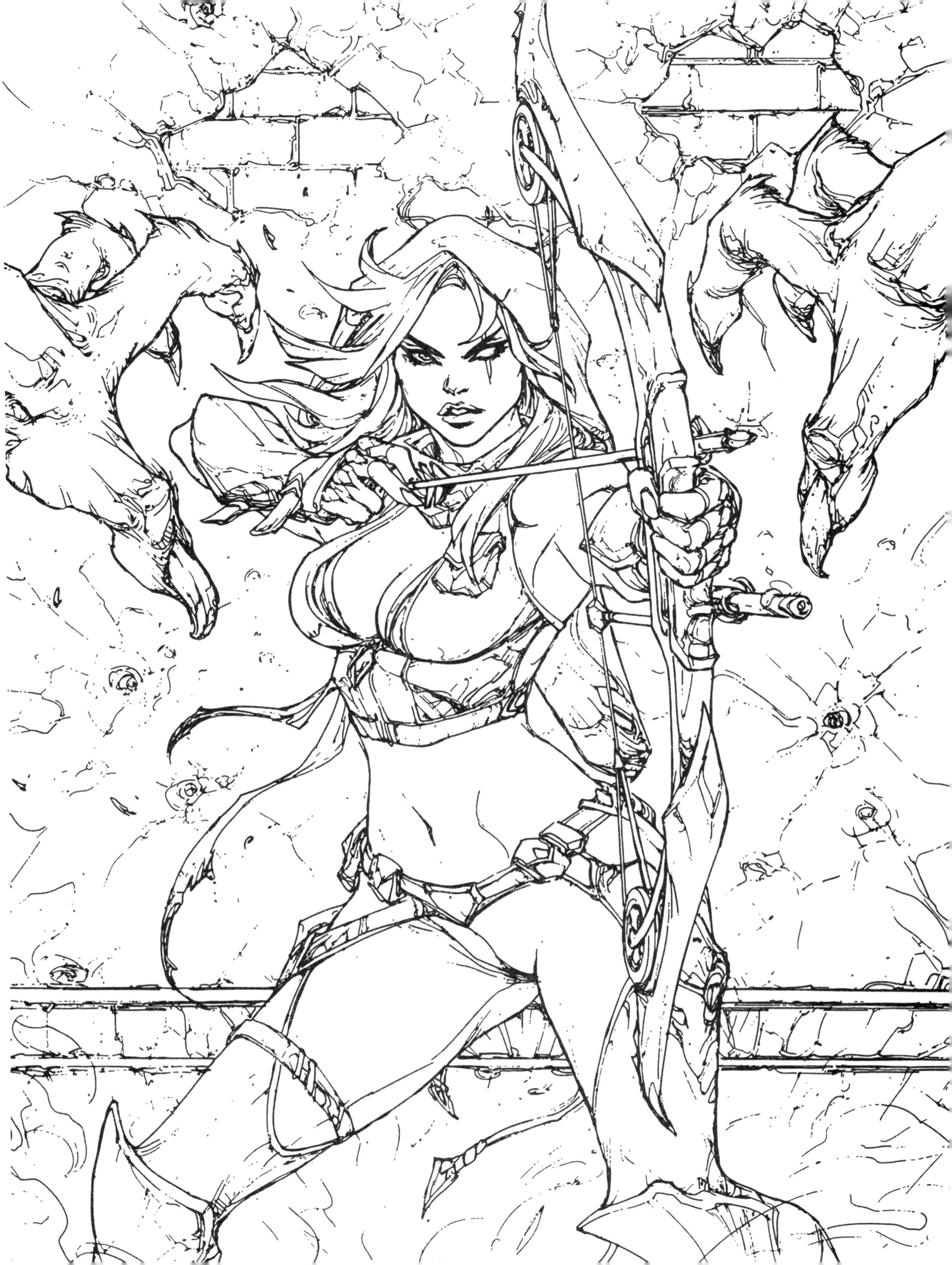

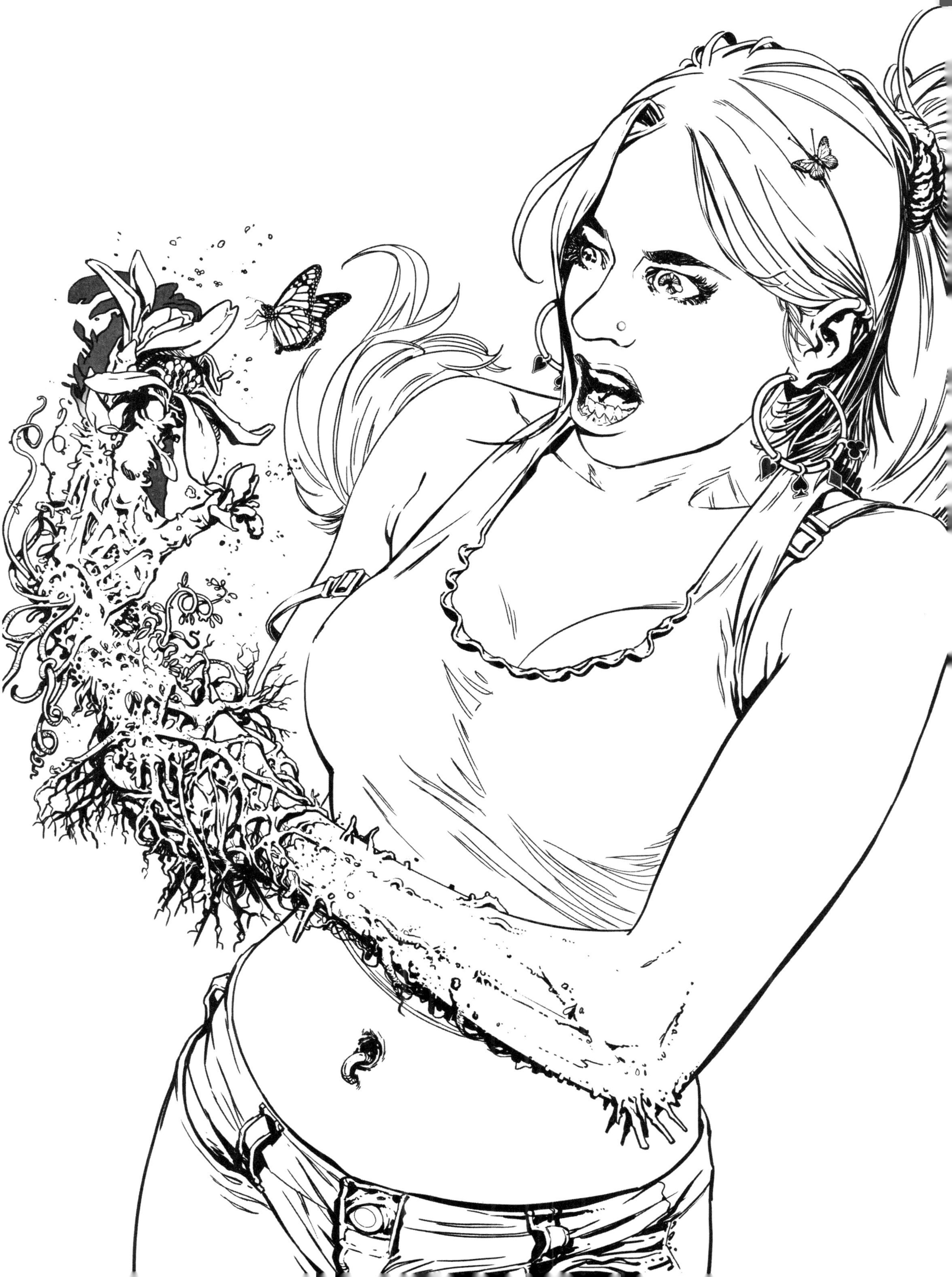

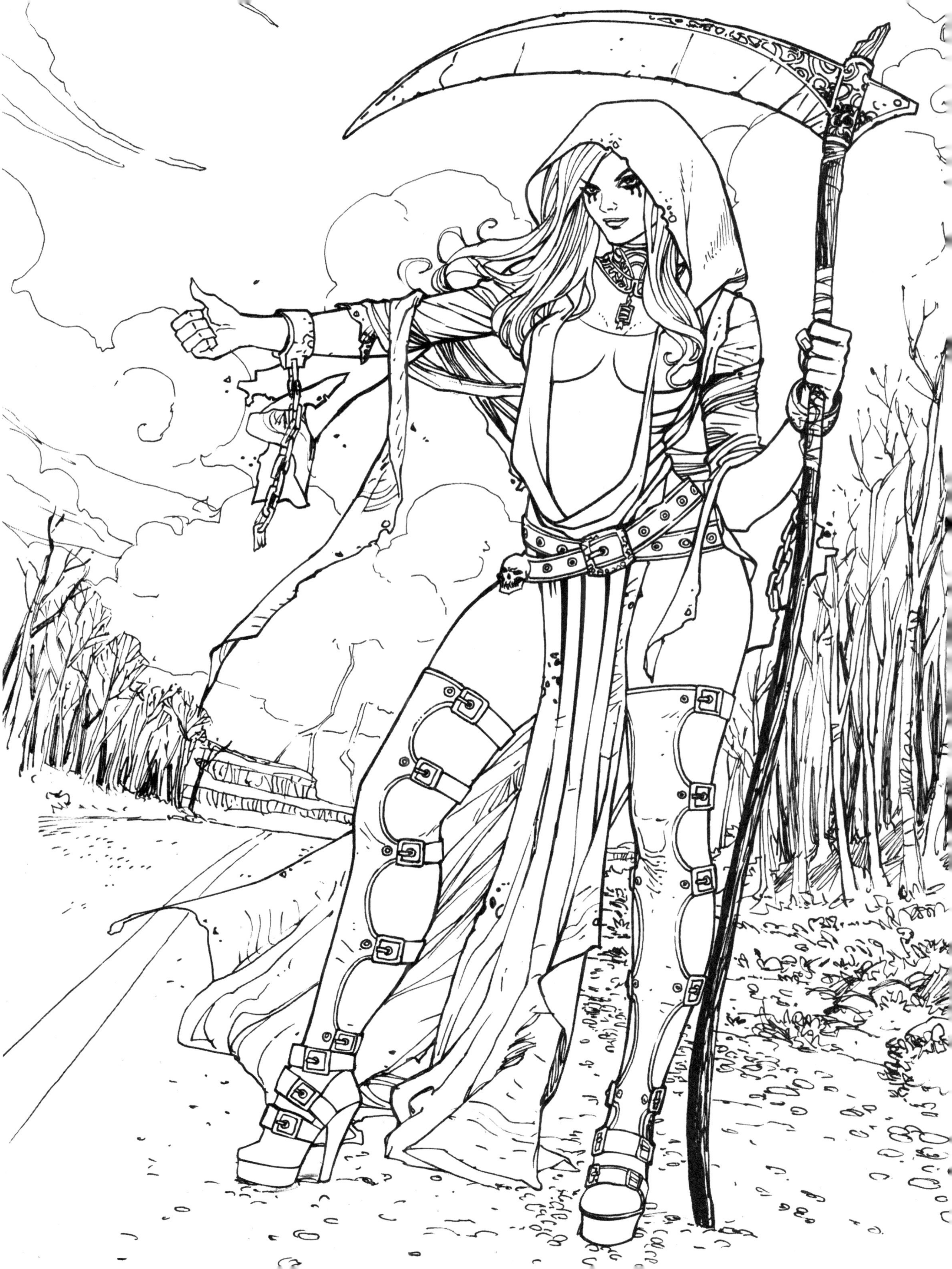

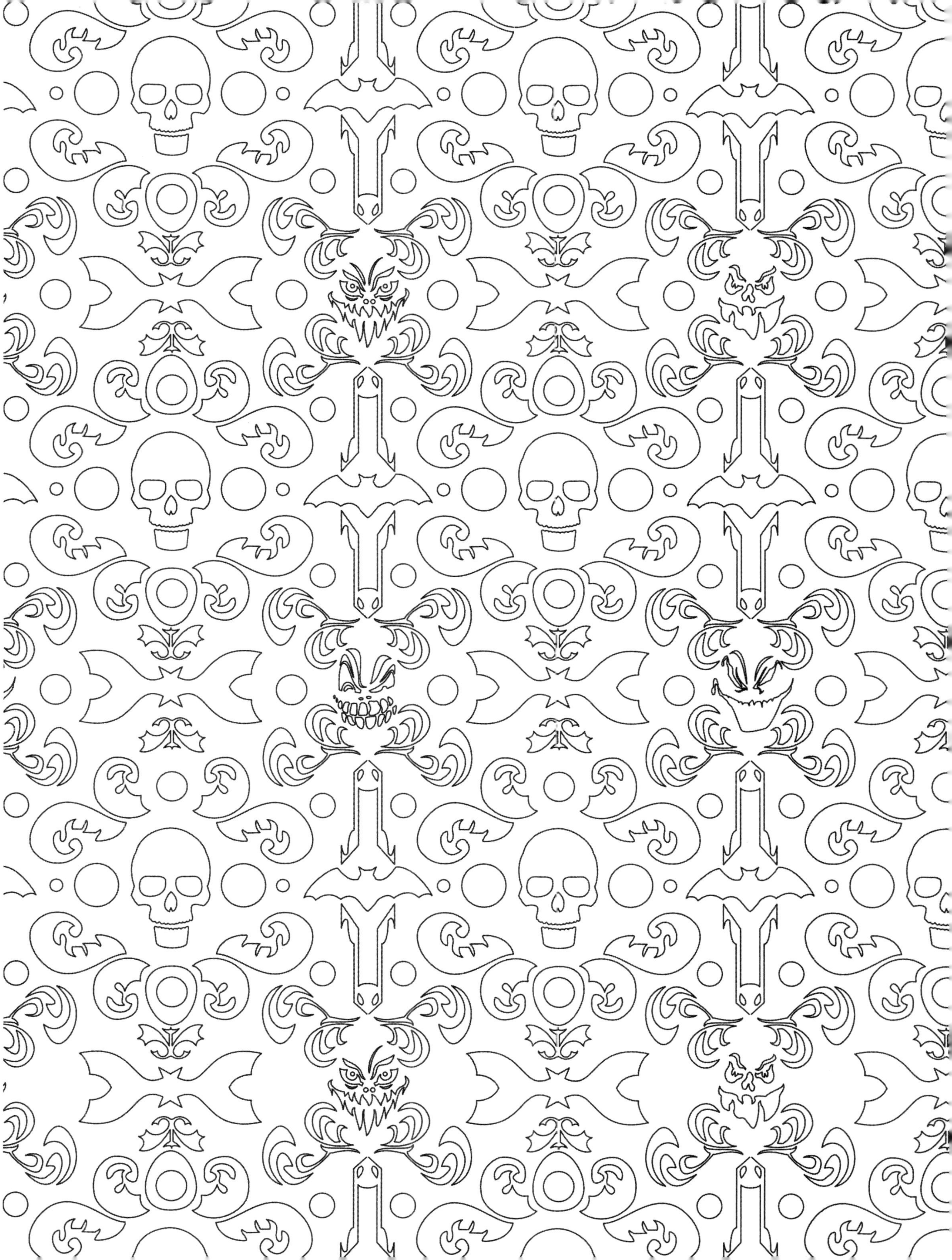

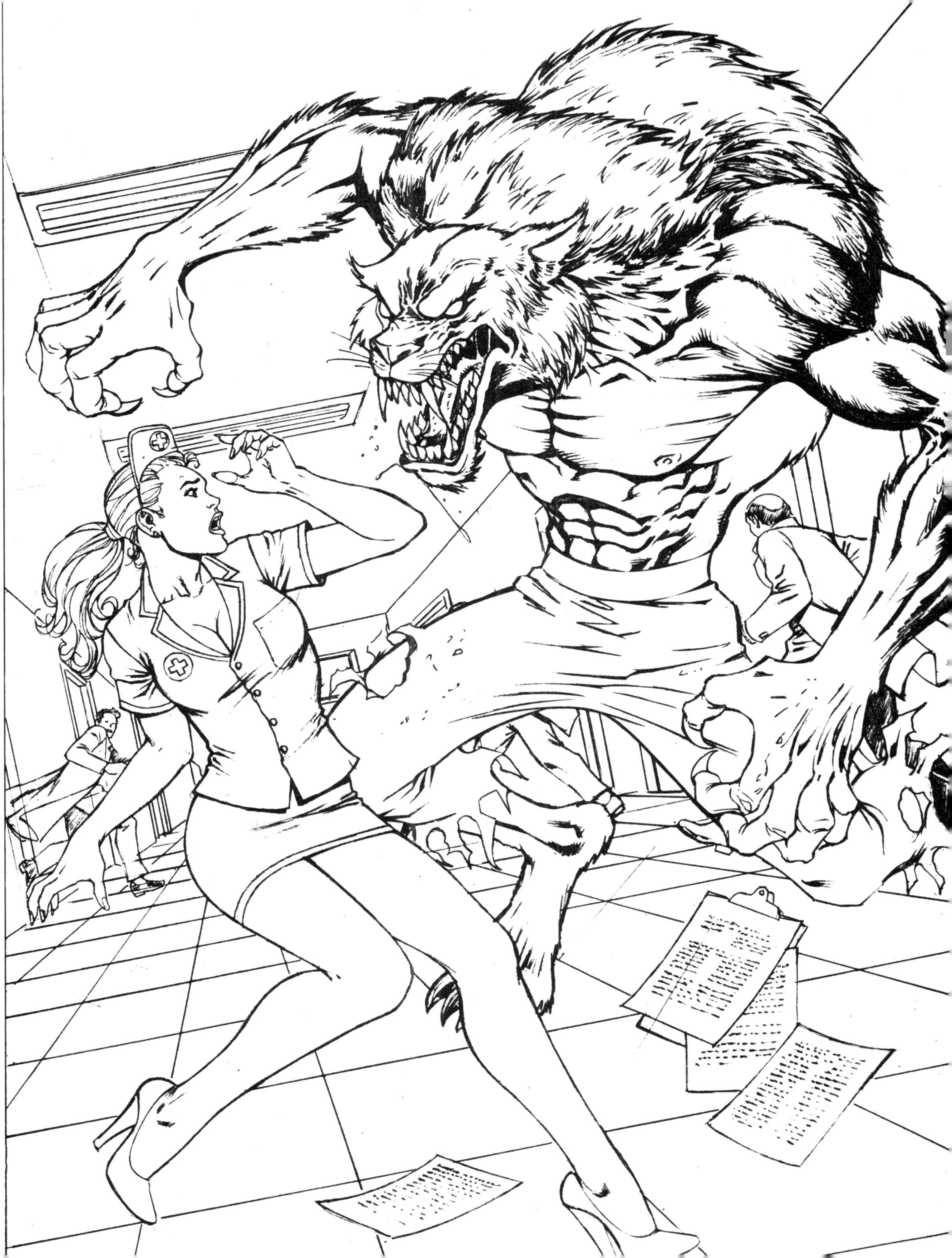

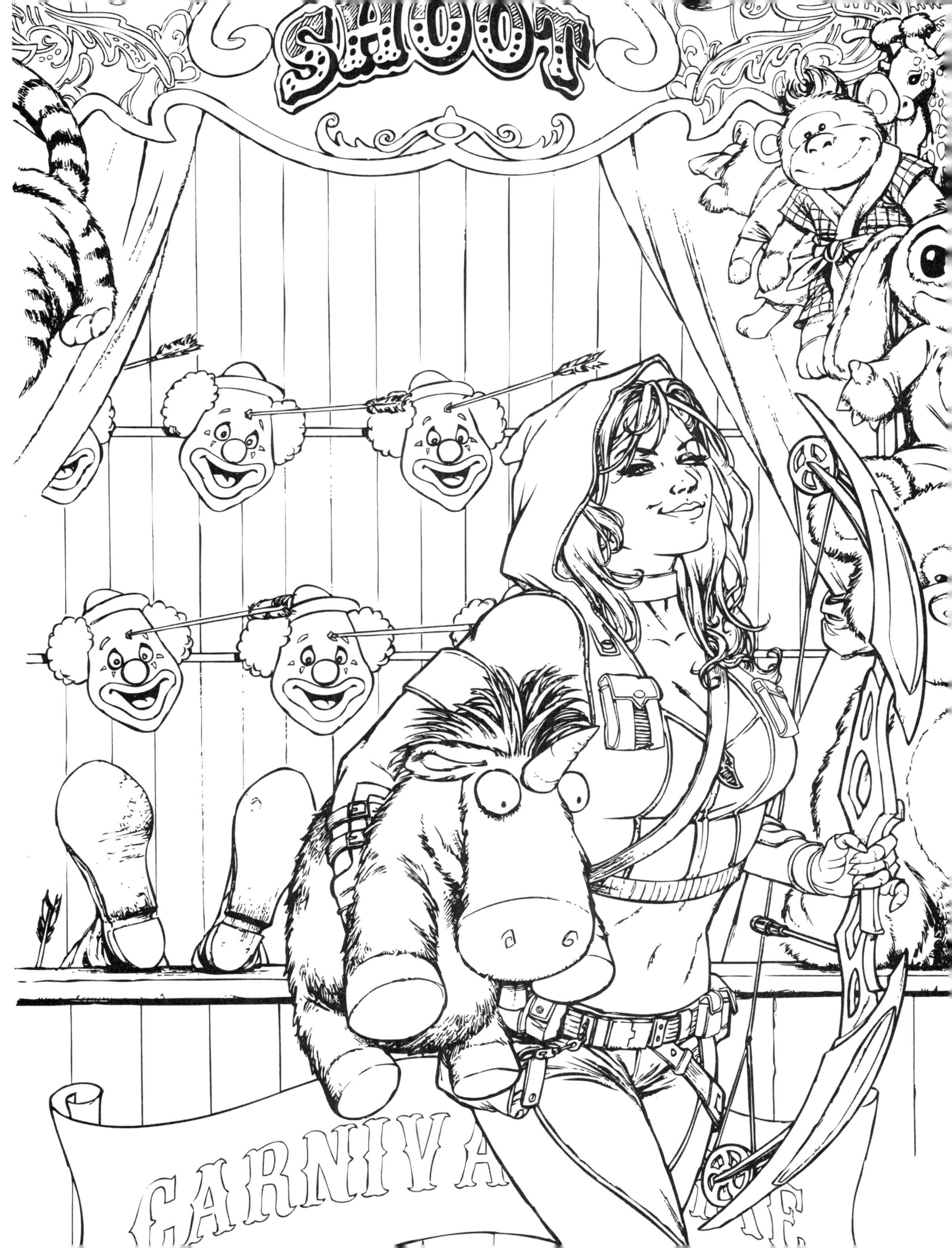
SHOOT
CARNIVA

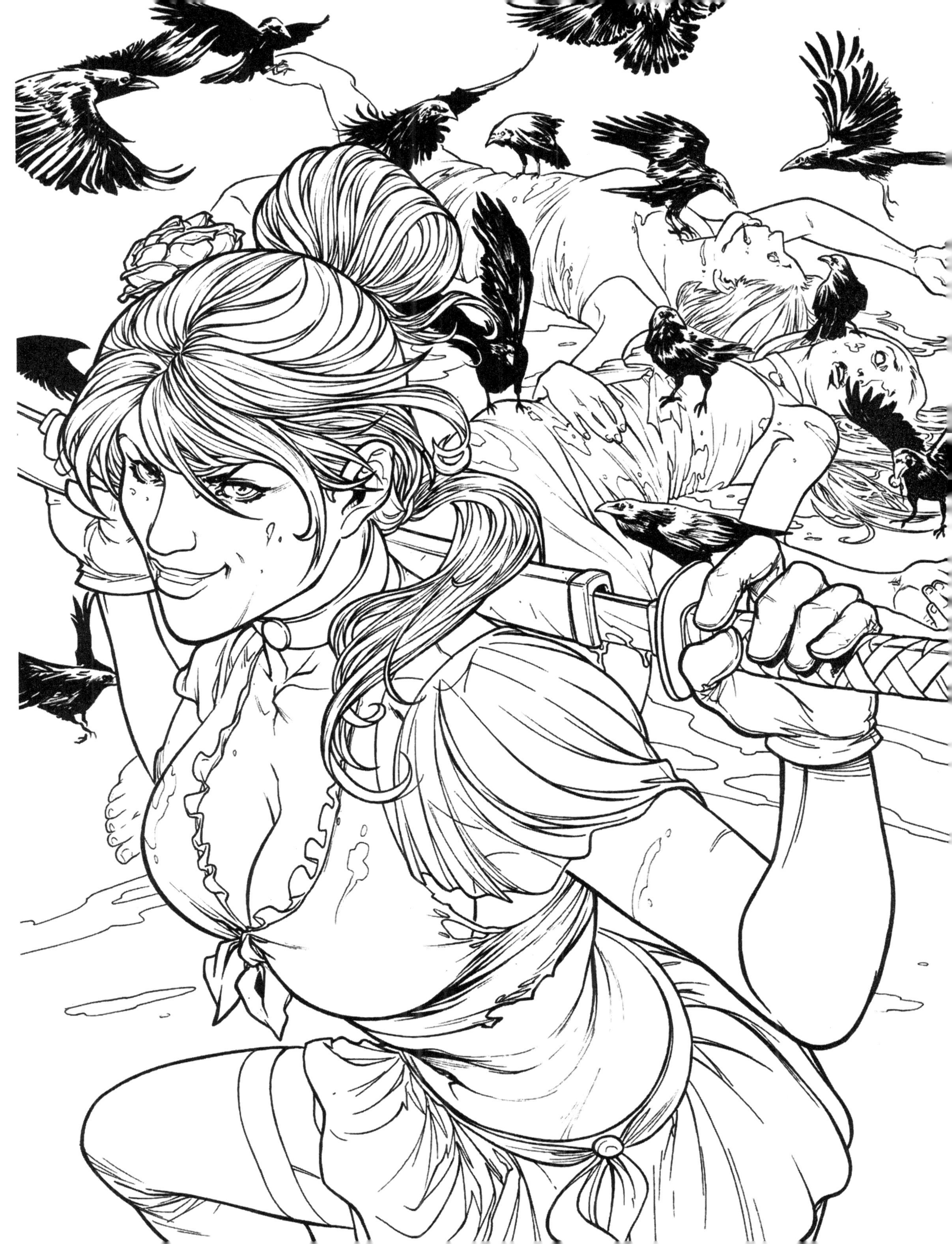

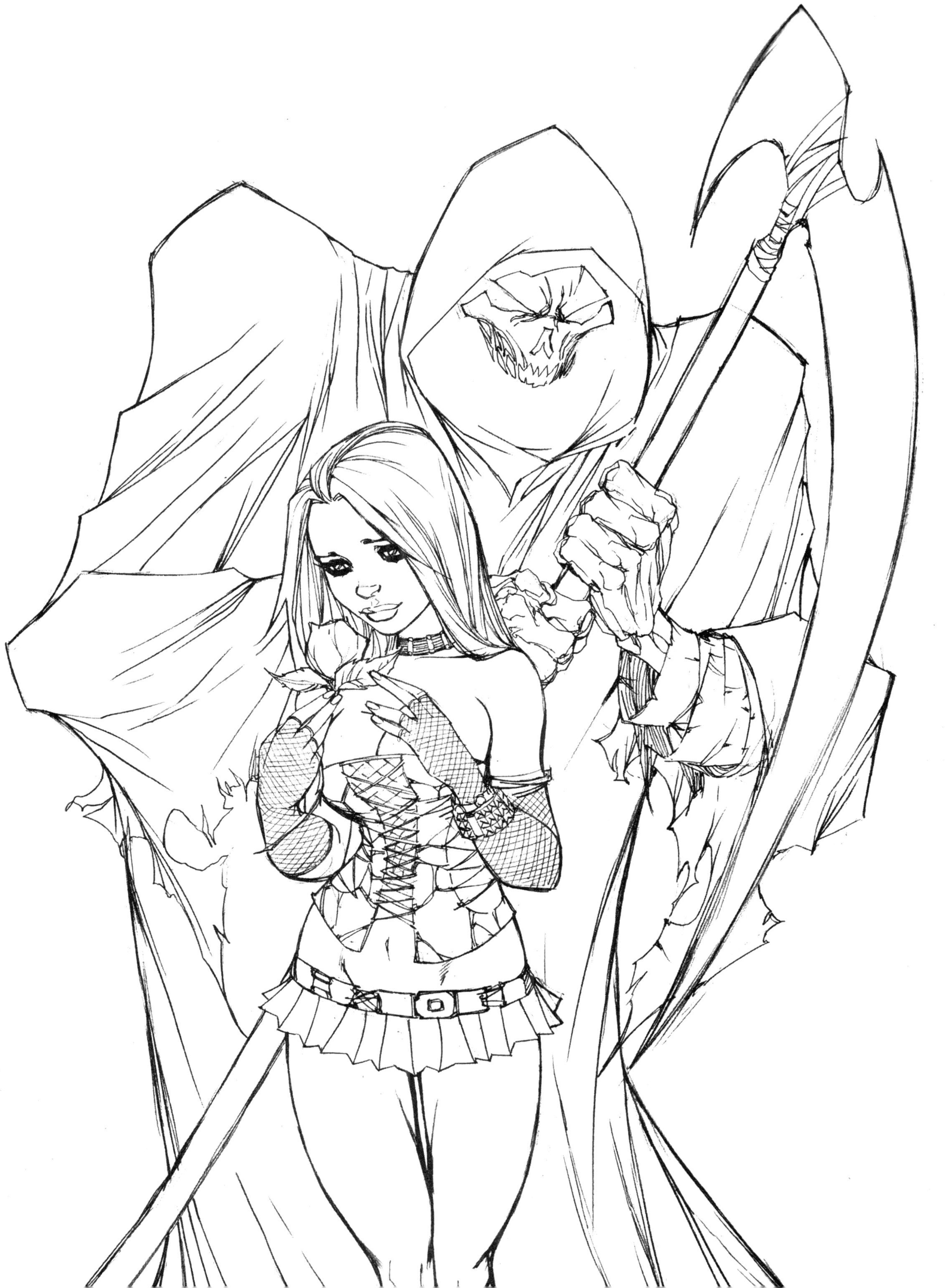

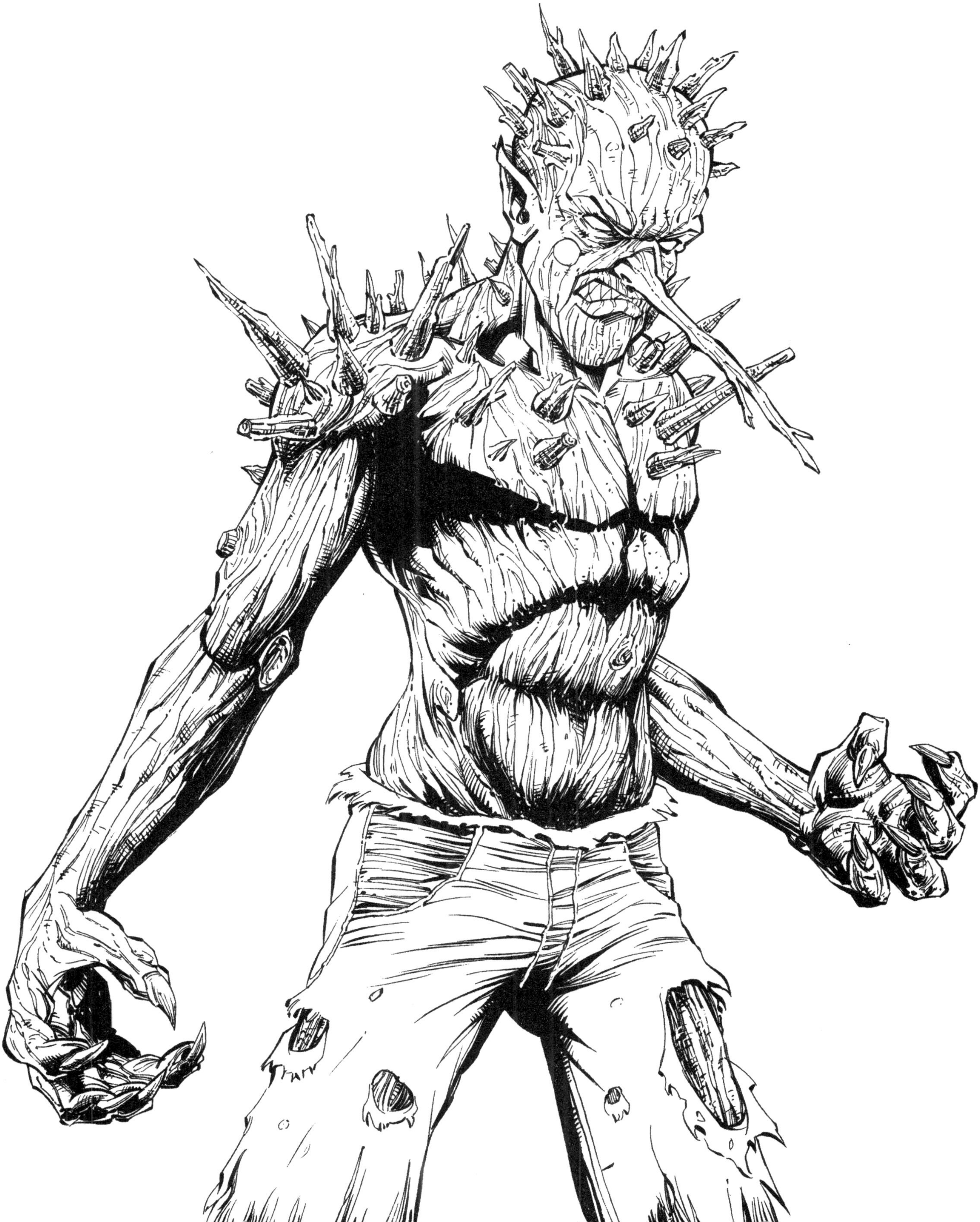

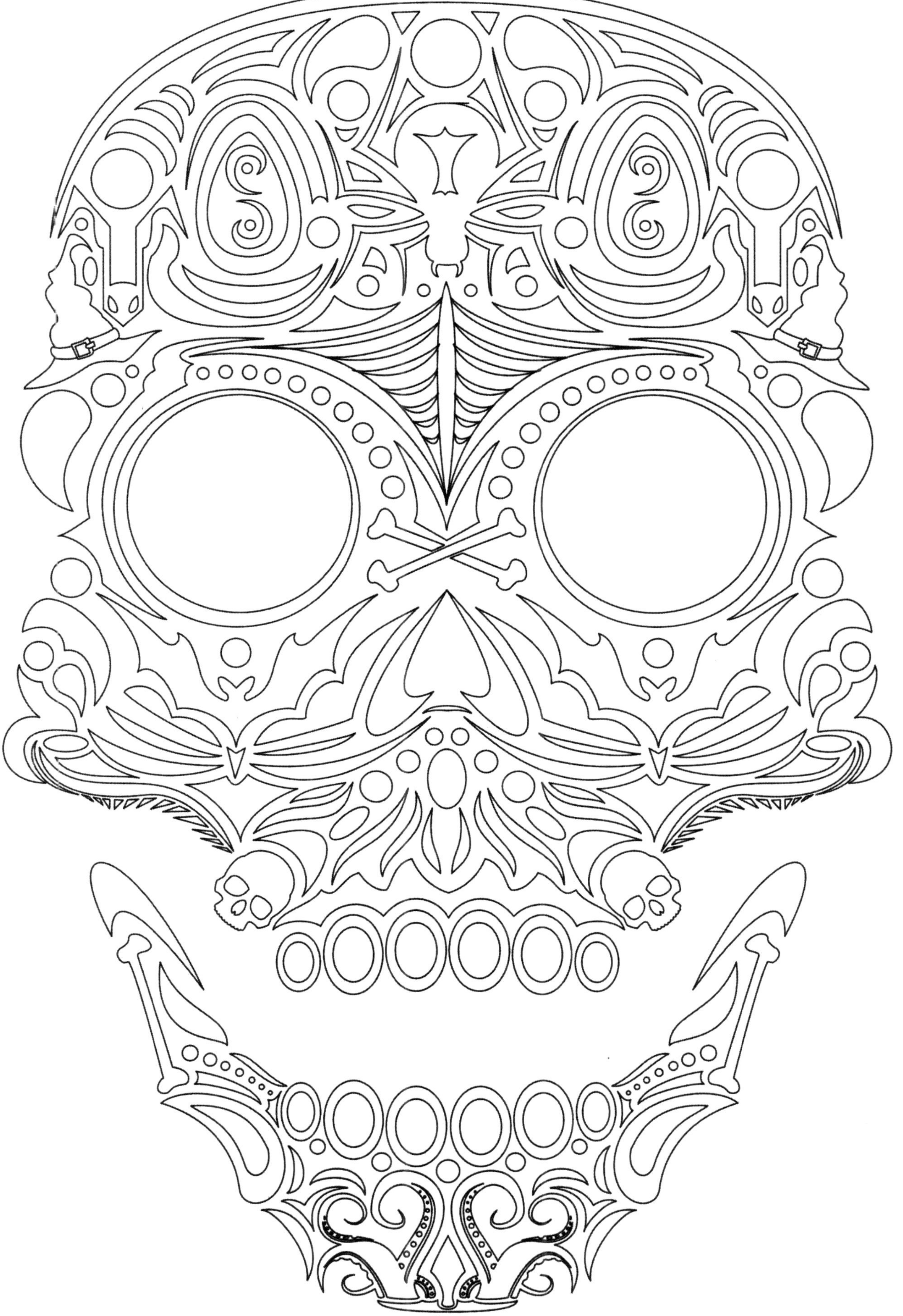

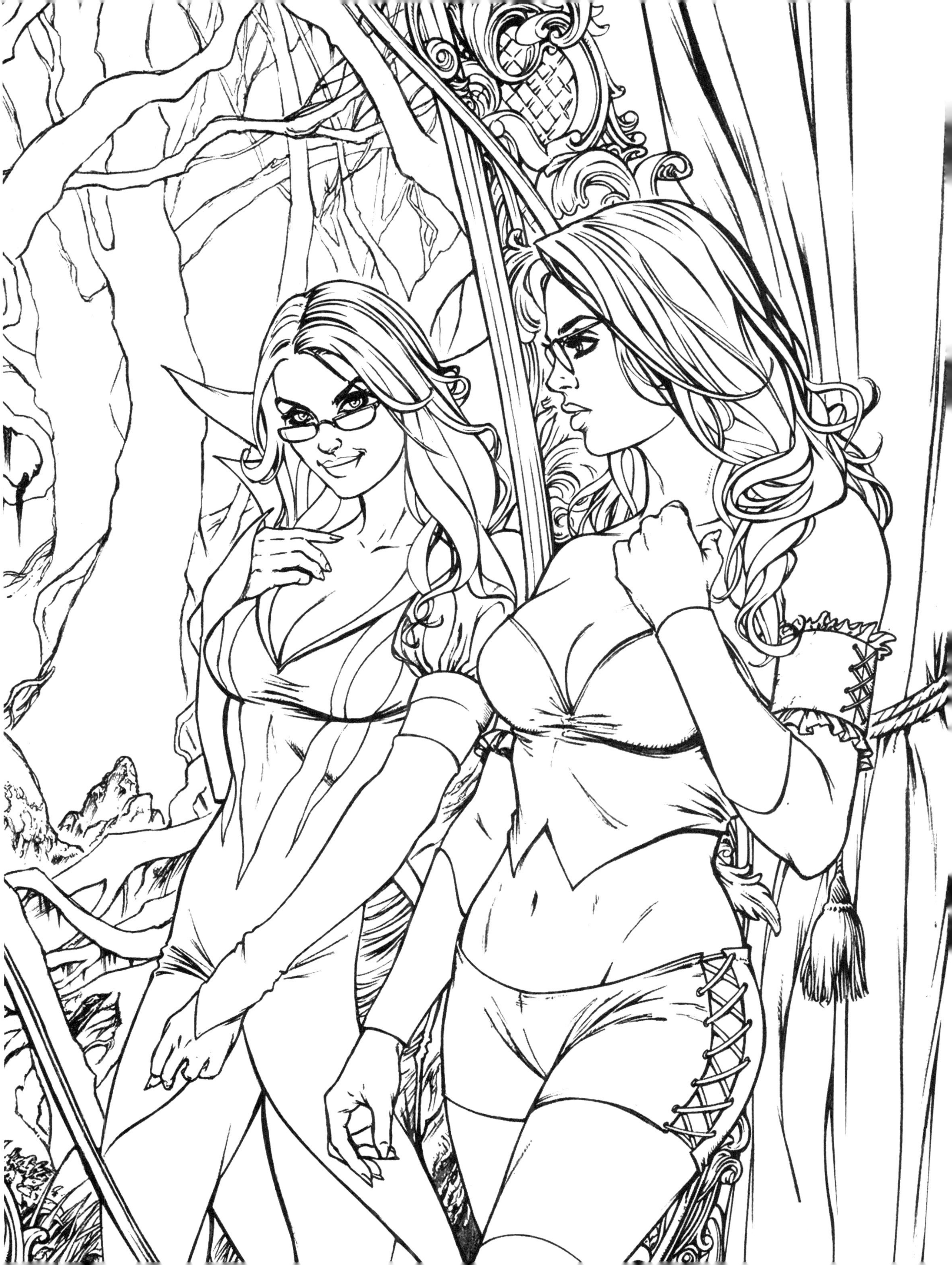

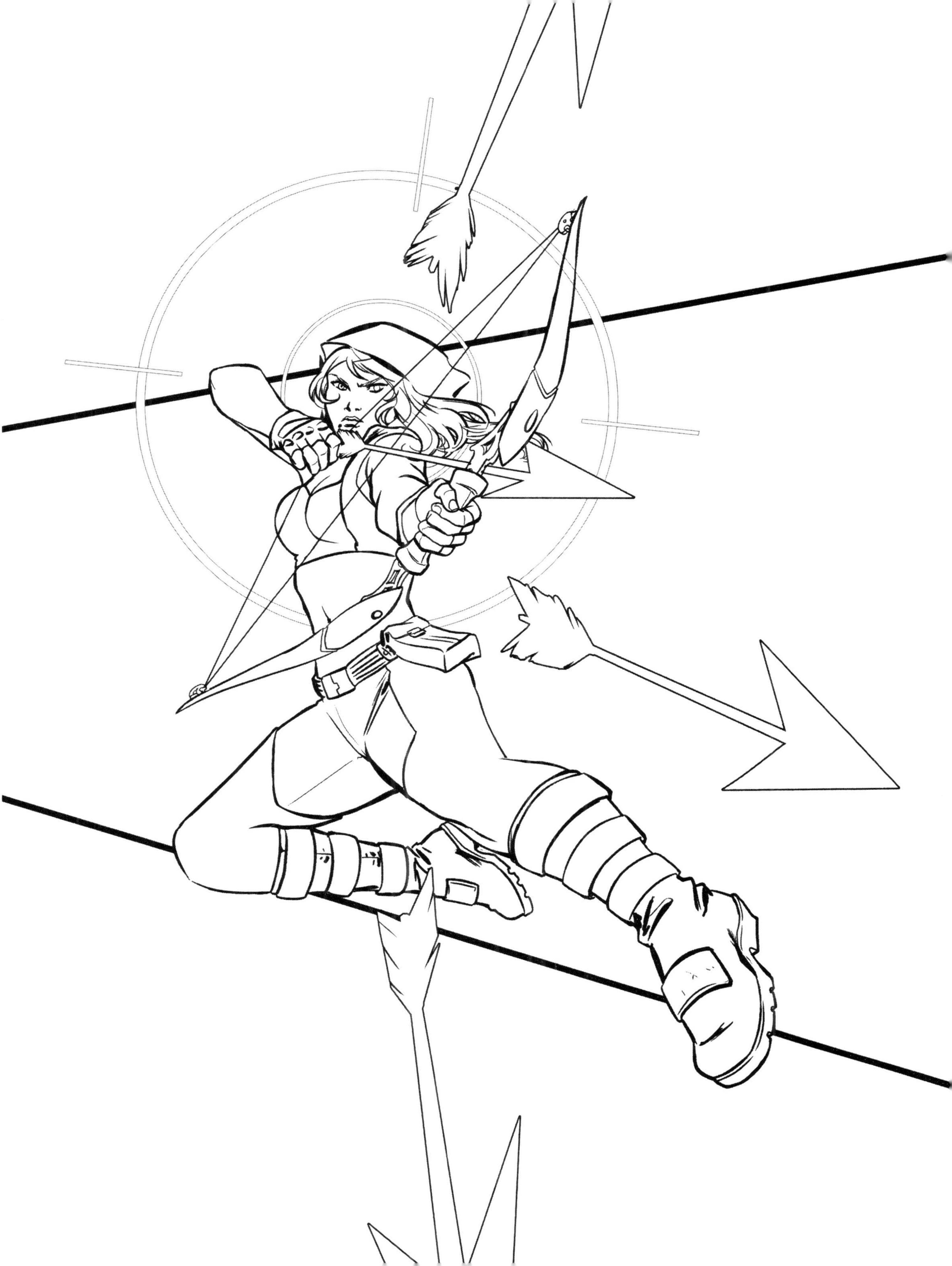

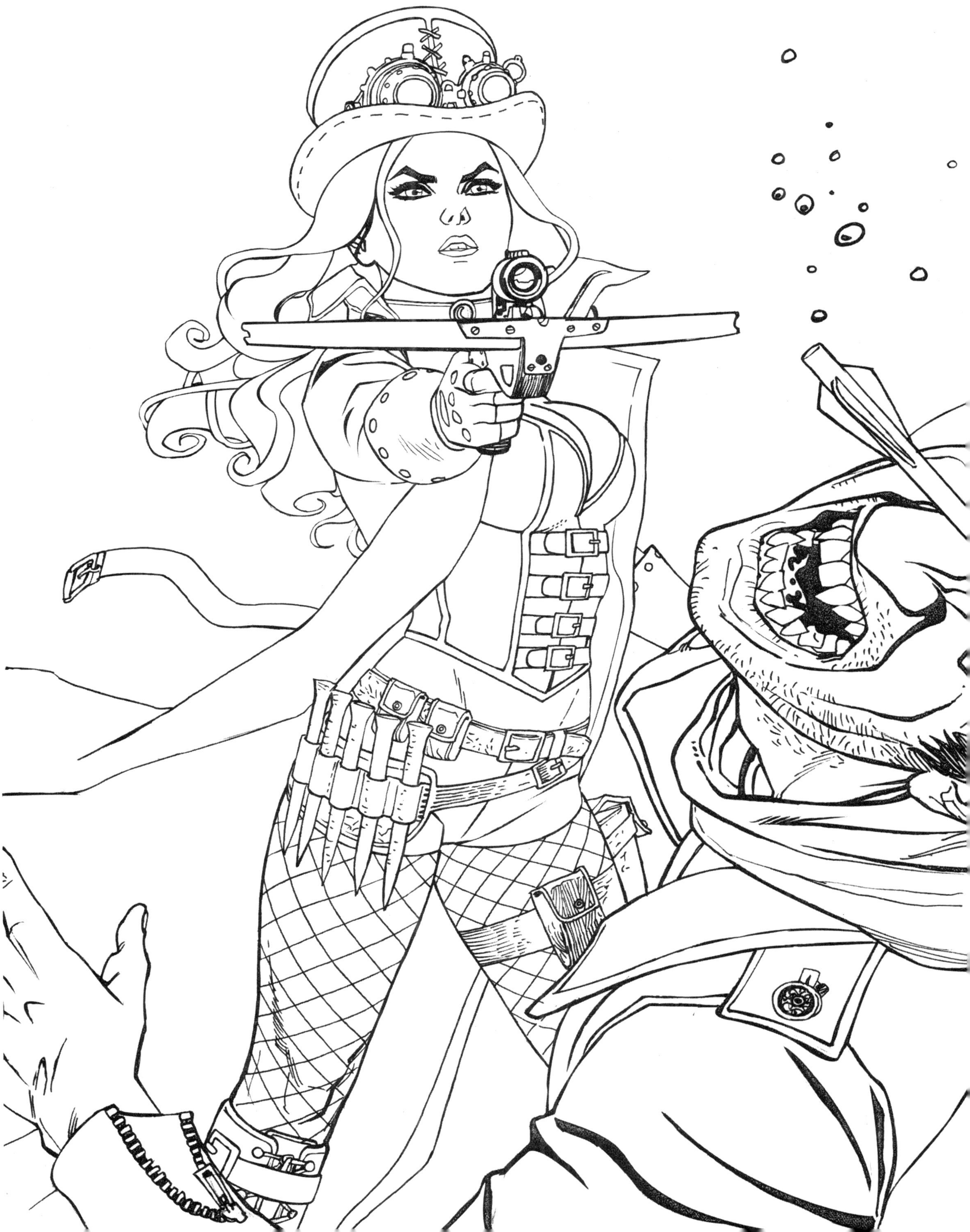

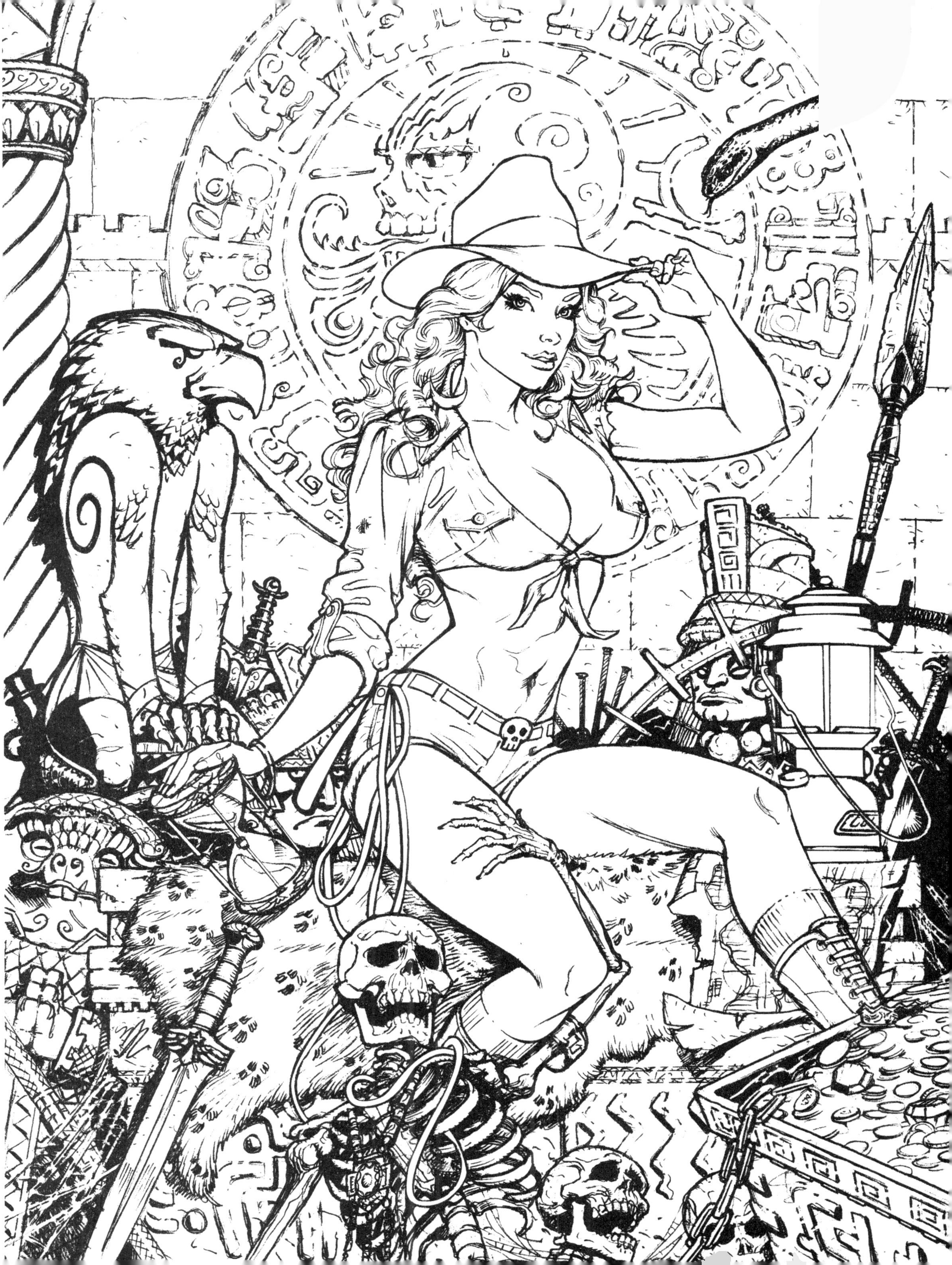

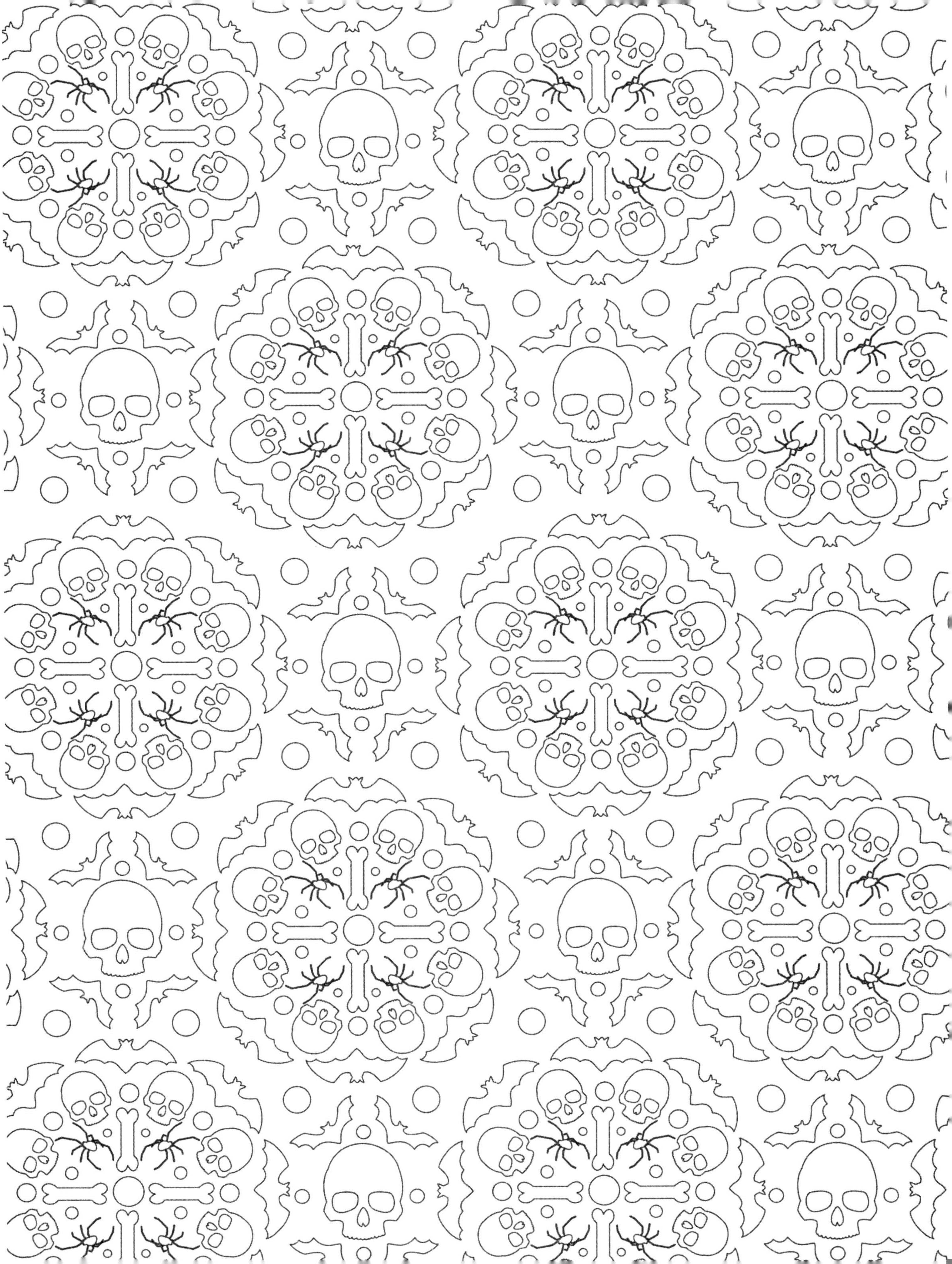

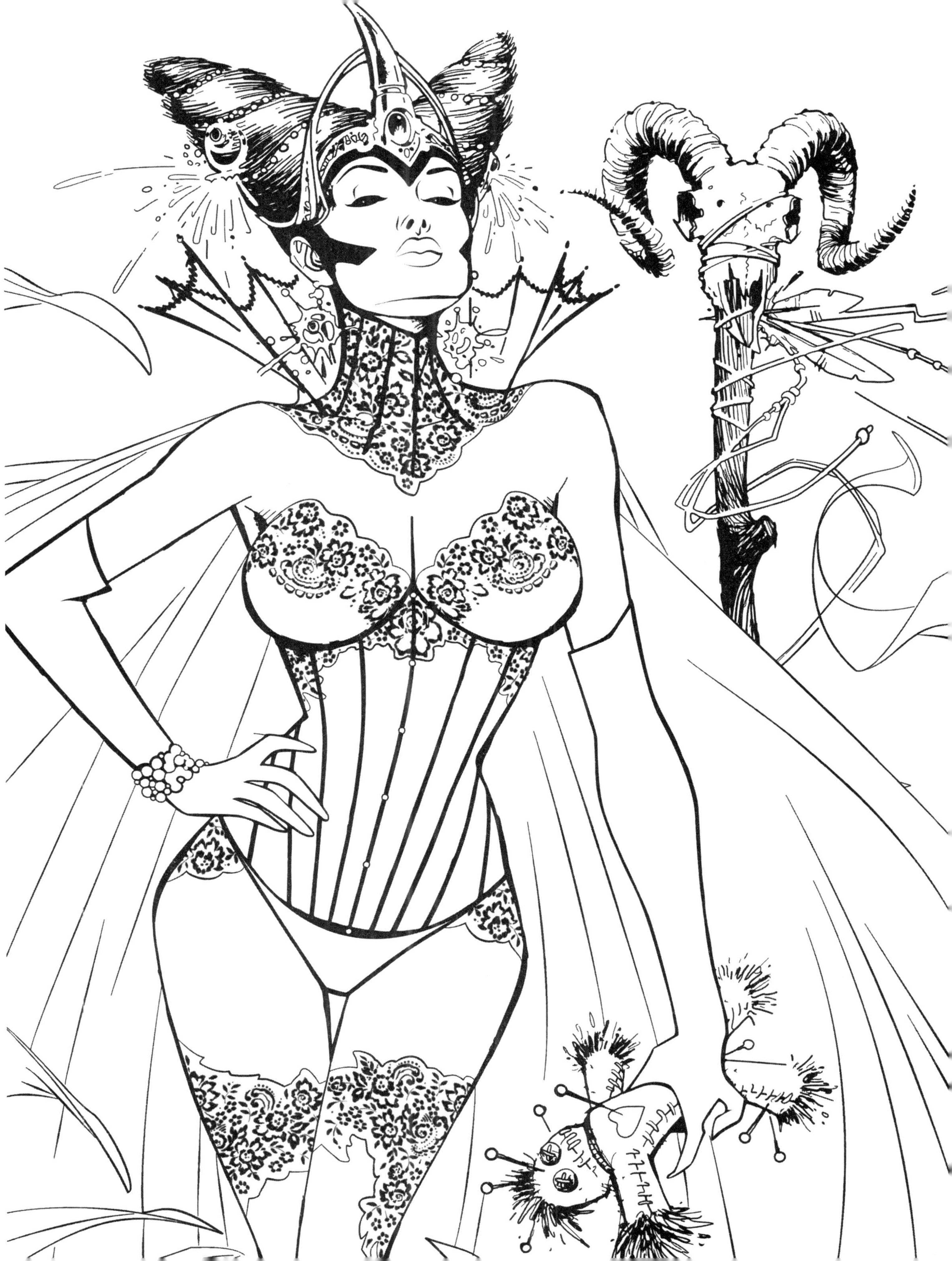

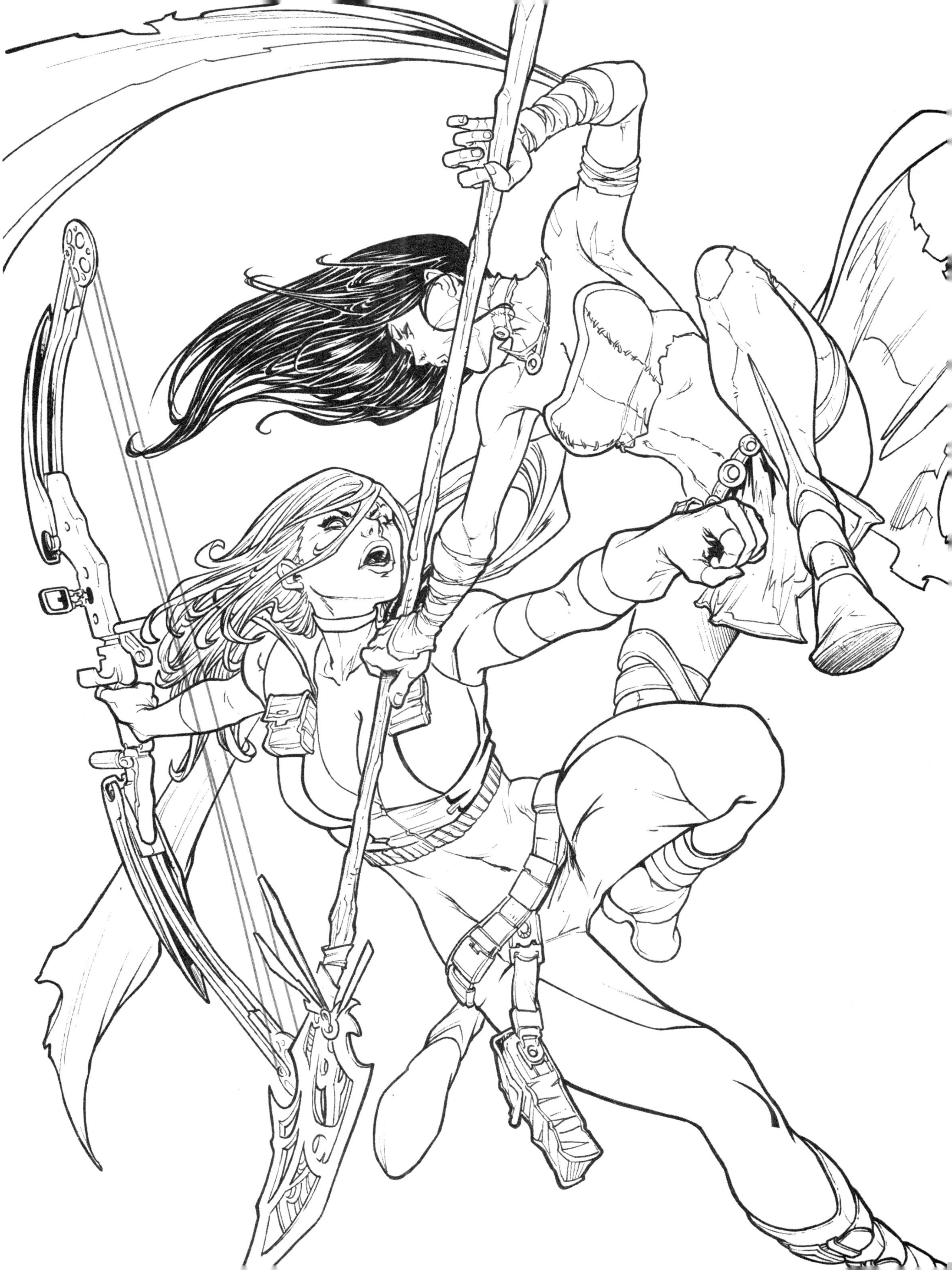

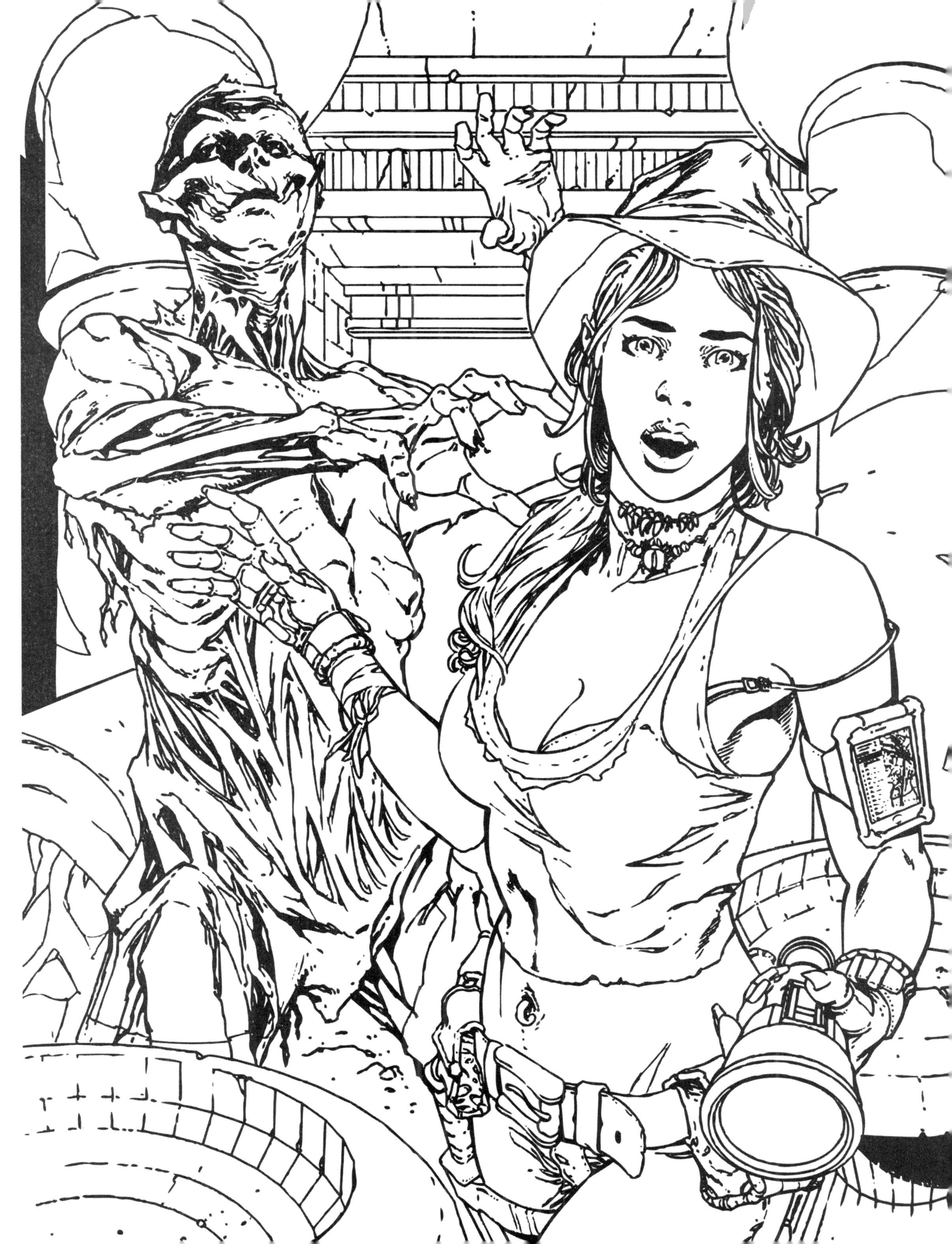

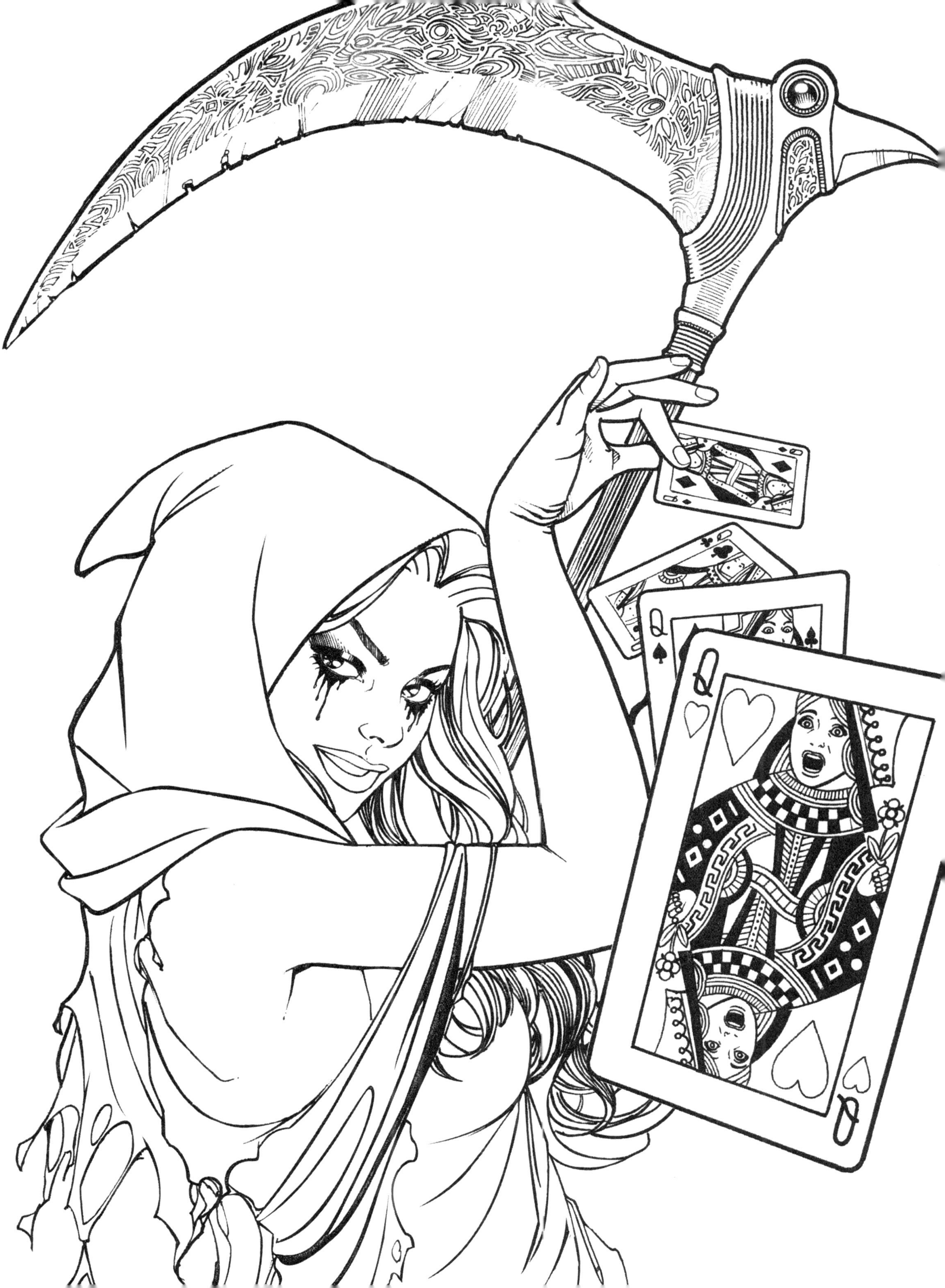

CONTINUE THE CREATIVITY WITH MORE ZENESCOPE COLORING BOOKS

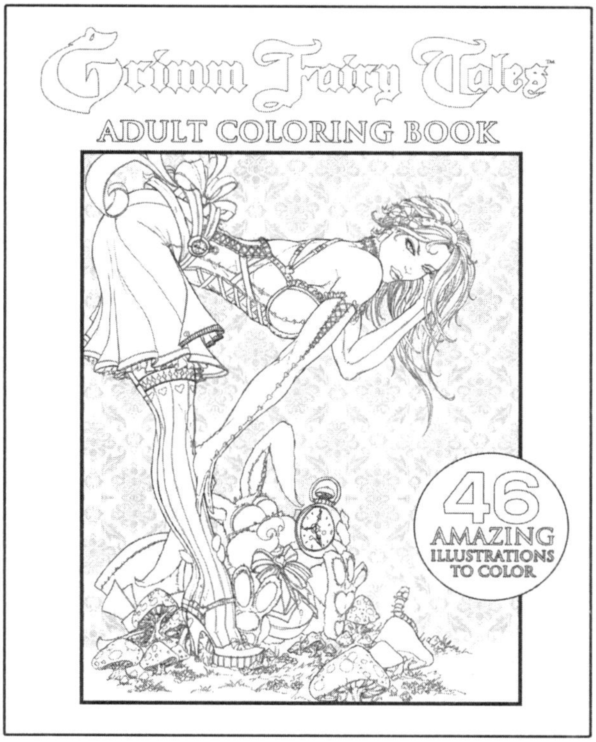
Grimm Fairy Tales
ADULT COLORING BOOK
46
AMAZING
ILLUSTRATIONS
TO COLOR

GRIMM FAIRY TALES
ADULT COLORING BOOK

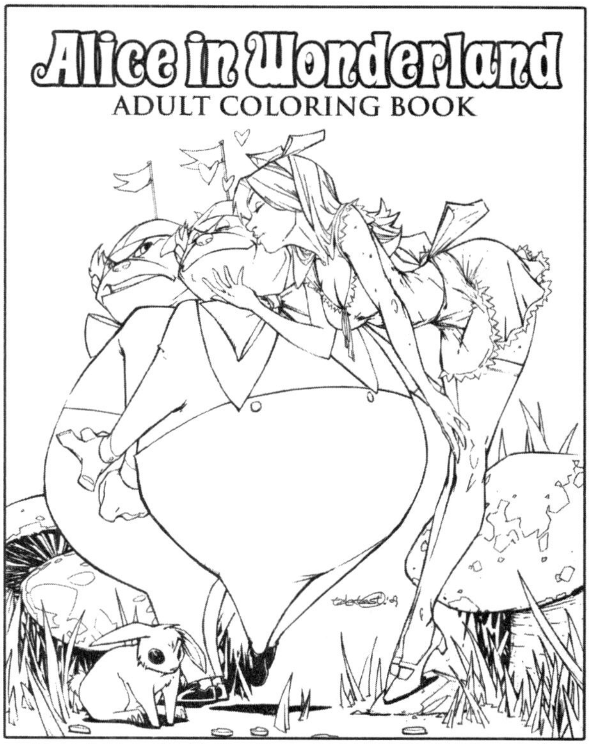
Alice in Wonderland
ADULT COLORING BOOK

ALICE IN WONDERLAND
ADULT COLORING BOOK

COLOR, RELAX, CREATE WITH ZENESCOPE'S ADULT COLORING KIT

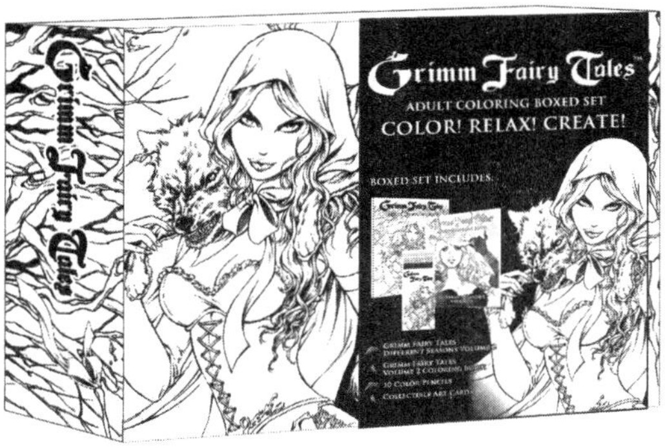
Grimm Fairy Tales
Grimm Fairy Tales
ADULT COLORING BOXED SET
COLOR! RELAX! CREATE!

INCLUDES:
2 COLORING BOOKS, 10 COLOR PENCILS & COLLECTIBLE ART CARDS

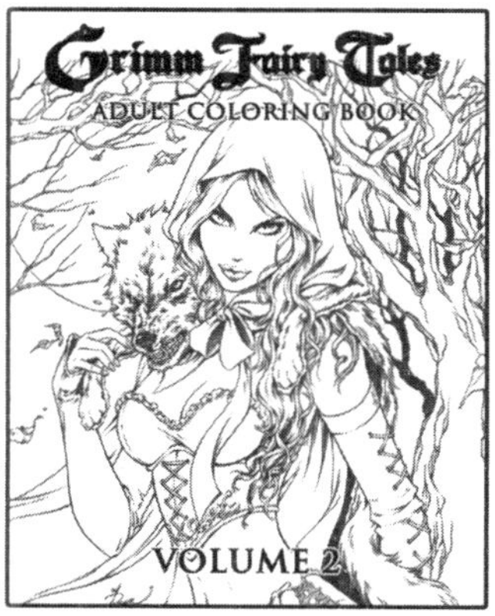
Grimm Fairy Tales
ADULT COLORING BOOK
VOLUME 2

GRIMM FAIRY TALES
ADULT COLORING BOOK
VOLUME 2

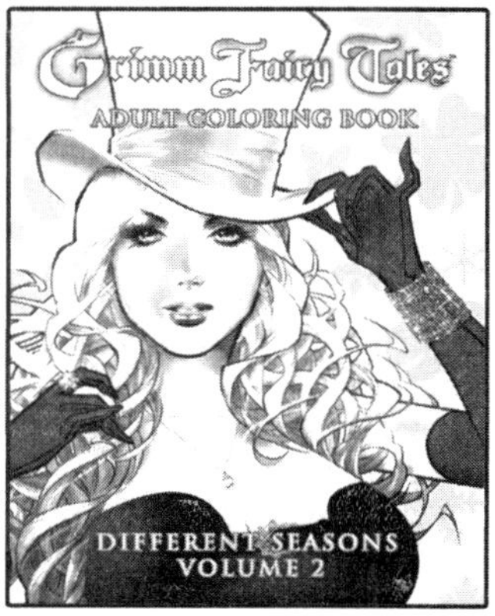
Grimm Fairy Tales
ADULT COLORING BOOK
DIFFERENT SEASONS
VOLUME 2

GRIMM FAIRY TALES
DIFFERENT SEASONS
VOLUME 2